JOCKEY TRAFFICKING

in
Blarnagosha

(Inc. The mysterious disappearance of Jacob Rees Mogg)

By

Michael Redmond

This story is set in the year 2028.

Bono is now President of Ireland and holds the distinction of being the second smallest President in the history of the Country and indeed of the World, standing at the mere height of 5ft 4" without a heal enhancement on his shoes. He claims that the Virgin Mary appeared to him in the gardens of Aras an Uachtarain and gave him an idea for a new song.

King Charles has gone slightly mad and tells everyone he meets that they smell of Weetabix.

Following the defeat of Russia in the war in Ukraine, Putin has resigned and accepted an offer to appear in the next series of "I'm a celebrity, get me out of here."

Keith Richards' is still alive.

Greta Thunberg claims she has achieved all she set out to do and will sing Sweden's entry in the Eurovision Song Contest this year…" Ding, Dong…. Ding Dong..Dock a Dick a Moo Moo."

None of these facts have anything to do or impact in any way with the events in Blarnagosha that year.

CHAPTER ONE

(Day One)

19th February 2028

Blarnagosha has been described as a small town just outside Ireland, and sometimes it is still chronicled as such. It is, in fact, inside Ireland but it is somewhat hidden away behind a large forest. Obviously, it can be reached by road, and you do not have to beat your way through the dark forest, possibly encountering some unlikely but intimidating local beast, in order to enter its domain. But it feels like it is tucked away from the rest of the world, which might in some way account for the unique personality traits of some of its residents. We come to Blarnagosha one week after the visit to Ireland of the newly crowned, Irish Pope, who had chosen the name, Pat, for his tenure as The Pontiff. Pope Pat 1st arrived back on the shores of Ireland on the 12th of October 2024. The people of the town of Blarnagosha and its nearby town, Poolavogue, had held high hopes that Pope Pat 1st might pass through their town in his Popemobile on his way to Galway. There were strong rumours that he was very keen to visit smaller communities and meet some of the people, rather than just hold a couple of big rallies in Dublin and Galway. Both communities had made huge efforts to present their towns in the best possible light to welcome Pope Pat 1st....flowers and garlands could be seen everywhere, some buildings were freshly painted, and both had erected huge banners on the entrances to their towns with the face of The Pontiff smiling out from them. However, the townsfolk of Blarnagosha became incensed when Pope Pat 1st chose to pay a visit to Poolavogue and had by-passed Blarnagosha.

In general, the visit of The Pontiff had passed smoothly enough, notwithstanding the fact that his cherished MITRE was either mislaid or stolen during his visit to Galway. Pope Pat was a man of simple tastes and pleasures who had been brought up on a council estate in Dublin with two parents who were referred to locally as a couple of 'rough diamonds'. If he succumbed to one vanity it was standing in front of a mirror and admiring the pomp of his MITRE atop his head, although he simply referred to it as 'me hat'. He still proudly maintained his broad Dublin accent and much of its dialect. He remembers placing his MITRE on a chair in the tented, backstage area after he'd just addressed a huge adoring crowd who'd turned up in their thousands to greet him. He'd taken his MITRE off because his head had become a bit sweaty from the television lights surrounding the stage area from where he'd quickly won over the assembled crowd and delivered an impassioned sermon for over an hour.

He'd casually strutted onto the stage, smiling and waving, as the crowd had cheered wildly. He'd stood for a few seconds without saying anything, merely stretching both arms outwards towards his audience in a gesture of embrace. He'd then pointed to all the television lights beaming down on him and said…

'Jaysus, it's hot up here, I could do with a pint.'

The crowd immediately erupted into paroxysms of laughter, applause and wild cheering which lasted over a minute before Pope Pat 1st, man of the people, could launch into the bones of his sermon.

Once he'd placed his MITRE on the chair backstage afterwards, he'd devoured a large plate of ham sandwiches which had always been and remained his favourite choice of food to eat for lunch, despite often being offered more exotic fare. He even still alluded to them in Dublinese as 'hang sangitches.' Having emptied the plate of sandwiches, washed down by a large bottle of red lemonade, drunk by the neck, he'd turned to retrieve his MITRE from the chair. The chair was empty and there was no sign of his MITRE.

" Wha!…where's me bleedin' hat gone?'.

A wide search was quickly conducted for the missing ecclesiastical headgear, but it was never recovered. A replacement was quickly commissioned but as far as Pope Pat was concerned it could never replace the MITRE which had been hand fashioned by his Aunt Betty who had once run her own Haberdasher's shop in Talbot Street in Dublin. He'd flown back to Rome the next day with a heavy heart.

Vasco Devine, 25 years old, is the local Garda Sergeant. He'd been christened Vasco at the behest of his father, Gem, the local family butcher. Gem had long been obsessed with the exploits of Vasco Da Gama, the famed Portuguese explorer, and had decided, long before he even met Vasco's mother, Bernadette, that his first-born son would bear the brunt of his obsession with the so named seafarer and be lumbered with the same name.

Description of Vasco: He appears at first sight to be very tall and gangly, but it is almost an optical illusion. He is in fact only 5ft 8in in height but seems taller as a result of his elongated legs. His legs are almost twice the length of his upper body, so disproportionately long that when he sits down in an armchair, he needs to spread his legs apart at the knees in order not to shield his face. He has an unfortunate habit of never properly closing his mouth. He is deluded, totally misguided, and at times fanciful, bordering on quixotic.

Vasco had tried on two occasions to change his name by deed poll. Not only had he tried but he had succeeded with ease on both occasions. The first time he'd changed his first name to Thomas was when he was just 19 years old.

However, despite informing his family, friends and locals that his name was now officially Thomas and no longer 'Vasco', no one appeared to take any notice and continued to greet him and refer to him by his birth name. There was, however, one exception to that rule. Noreen Halligan, a local girl who worked in the local Post Office and who held out hopes of a romantic liaison with Vasco one day, had immediately agreed to call him Thomas. However, the manner in which she pronounced the name, Thomas, began to grate on Vasco quite quickly. She had an unfortunate tendency to linger on the 's'at the end of his name when she spoke it, which at times often progressed in a short sibilant whistle. After three weeks or so, Vasco politely requested that she revert to 'Vasco' like everybody else. The second time he'd changed his name by deed poll was three years or so later. He felt he was now more mature to make such a decision and that others would be more likely to accord him some respect this time. However, no one ever saw him as a 'Sebastian', not even Noreen. So, he accepted his fate that when the time came, the name 'Vasco', would most likely be inscribed on his gravestone.

Vasco's father, Gem, runs the local family butcher's and since what he describes as 'the bloody infernal rise of vegetarianism', he has held a deep dislike of the culture and at one point ludicrously refused to eat vegetables as a form of protest to anyone who declined the pleasure of eating meat. However, once his protest failed to gain any momentum after just a few weeks, he no longer baulked at the sight of a vegetable on his dinner plate as long as it was accompanied by a momentous helping of meat. His deep love of meat sometimes inspires him to write poetry on the subject.

"A shank of spring lamb
only £10 per kilogram
A joy to behold
Of pleasures untold."

Description of Gem: Gritty of face. He is proud of the fact that he has never worn gloves in his life and harbours a deep distrust of anyone who does wear them. He has a strong dislike of umbrellas, musicals, sandals, and any daytime TV presenter, and claims to have despised vegetarianism from birth. He needs spectacles but flatly refuses to wear them.

Once went to Manchester.

Vasco feels embarrassed about the fact that he still lives at home with his father and mother at the age of twenty-five. It was for this reason that he has placed a ladder permanently against the side of the house which gives him access directly into his bedroom on the upper floor by climbing in through the window.
He only ever enters the house by this route. He feels it accords him some degree of independence from his parents and has convinced himself that he does, in fact, live in his own flat, despite having to 'share' the bathroom and sitting room with his 'flat mates' who just happened to be his parents.

Roisin Dunphy works part time in the local Garda station as an administrative assistant to Vasco. It is just an unpaid summer job as she is studying law in Dublin the rest of the time and is only doing it to pass the time. However, on the insistence of Vasco, her job title had been now upgraded to PA to the Garda Sergeant. Roisin had just taken a call from the local pub owner, Peadar Scully, that his pub had been broken into during the night and a number of things, in particular the entire stock of cigarettes had been stolen from the cigarette machine. Vasco had not yet arrived at the station, so she rang him on his mobile phone to inform him of the incident. He was having breakfast at home with his parents when he took the call.

'Have to go', Vasco said as he stood up from the breakfast table, 'been a heist in the bay area at Peadar Scully's'.

'Oh, a heist, isn't that exciting...no one better to deal with a heist than my Vasco', intoned his mother, Bernadette, supportively.

'A heist is it, be Jesus, a heist in Blarnagosha', his father laughed sarcastically, 'you'd better get the FBI involved before it gets out of hand'.... a feckin' heist...should we all stay indoors until it blows over in case they take hostages to make a getaway'.

Vasco ignored his father's playful taunting and rushed out the door to make his way to the Garda station en route to the scene of 'the heist'.

'I didn't know there was a bay area in Blarnagosha?', Bernadette said after Vasco had departed.

'There isn't', his father replied, 'he's just aping that gobshite, Horatio, from Miami Vice, he's talking about the pond beside Peadar Scully's pub.

Description of Bernadette: Pleasant of face. She is so often seen wearing an apron that when you meet her not wearing one, you sense something is missing. Despite a homely demeanour, she possesses an underlying air of self-determination. Like her husband, Gem, she has only travelled outside of Ireland once. She accompanied her sister, Angela, who had stunted growth in her left arm to Lourdes seven years ago in the hope of a miracle cure. However, in some way, two miracles occurred. Firstly, her sister's arm did start to grow to a normal length but unfortunately it didn't stop there...it kept growing to an abnormally long length to the extent that it is now almost twice as long as her right arm. Angela returns to Lourdes every year in the hope that her arm will retreat to a normal length, but any further miracle has eluded her up to now.

Vasco was en route on foot to Peadar Scully's pub which was only a couple of hundred yards from his house when he met Jacko, a retired jockey who lives in an area of Blarnagosha known as Jockeytown.

Jockeytown isn't really a town in itself as it is comprised mostly of a couple of streets at the end of the town.
Jockey Town is home to over 30 retired jockeys, mostly of Irish nationality but jockeys of all nationalities are welcome to set up home there. Jockeytown was the brainchild of Jacko, one of Ireland oldest and longest serving jockeys, although it is difficult to find any record of Jacko riding a winner across the finishing line in any annals of horse racing memorabilia. In short, Jacko was very popular among his fellow jockeys, due to a combination of his cheerful disposition and the fact that none of them ever envisioned him overtaking them on his horse as they all galloped towards the finishing line in a race. It is a self - sufficient area of no more than 2 square miles, consisting of around 40 homes, a few shops, including one specialising in designer jockey ware. All the buildings in Jockeytown were designed to dimensions to suit the smaller statures of the jockey population, even though the partners of some of the jockeys are not vertically challenged.

The idea for creating Jockeytown came to Jacko in the early 1980's when a fellow jockey had suffered serious injuries as a result of an encounter with one of those small electric, street cleaning machines with a circular rotating brush to the front commonly used by the Council. The Council employee in charge of the said machine had claimed that he hadn't spotted the slightly built jockey over the rim of the vehicle when he'd stepped off the pavement to cross the road.

'Ah Vasco, the very man. I was about to call into the station to talk to you about somethin' I heard on the grapevine…. a very serious matter.'

'I can't talk to you now, Jacko, I'm on my way to investigate a heist.'

'Be God, a heist!'

'And I'll have to ask you in future that when you're addressing me in an official capacity, it needs to be, 'Sergeant'.'

'Right you be…. Sergeant, I'll call into the station later so.'

'Should be back in a couple of hours…unless I need to execute an immediate pursuit of the culprit.'

'Right so…. oh, before you go, do ye happen to have a light on you, Serg…or do I just call you, Vasco?… cos' it's not too official like.'

'No, I don't have a light on me…see you later.'

CHAPTER TWO

Donie Griffin, presides over the local town Council. The word 'presides' is perhaps a little grandiose in the circumstances in that he is the only member of the Council. His greatest pride is that the town, under his leadership, has won the much vaunted, West of Ireland tidy town competition for two years in a row.

Description of Donie Griffin: He is a small, squat man in his mid-fifties with a rambling beer belly which would ramble more precariously were it not tucked behind tight fitting shirts whose buttons were hard pressed to contain it. He has a long, sharp nose with a lengthy, single wisp of hair growing out from the middle of it. The wisp of hair is long enough to catch the wind and flutter according to which direction it is blowing.

Donie likes to rise at 6.30 every morning and take a brisk, pre-breakfast walk through the town, admiring the abundance of floral displays dotted throughout the town. He would sometimes stop to sit for a while in joyful contemplation on the outside wall of a fountain he had commissioned to be installed in a small area of greenery on the outskirts of the town. He had arranged for a couple of blossom trees to be planted aside the fountain, according it a measure of 'far eastern exotica'. He is convinced that the fountain had swung the vote in his favour against competitors when the judges had sat down to decide each previous year on the winner of the tidiest town. This year, he had arranged for a heated fishpond to adjoin the fountain, populating it with colourful species of fish and vegetation.

It was to his utter consternation that when he arrived at the fountain this morning, he'd found that both blossom trees lay bent and twisted on the ground, all the surrounding flowers had been uprooted, the fish lay dead, floating on the surface of the pond, and the walled area around the fountain had been daubed with paint.

'Damn vandals', he screamed at the top of his voice. He was both incensed and heart-broken at the same time as he viewed the carnage in front of him. As his shout echoed around him, the former Garda Sergeant of the town, Seamus Gilfuddy, was riding past on his motorcycle sidecar. You could say that Seamus Gilfuddy had retired but he had simply walked out of the Garda station one day last year muttering the words, 'can't be bothered anymore', repeatedly as he passed people on the street...'no crime ever happens here anyway'

He was 65 at the time and had just reached pensionable age, making him eligible for the State pension.

Description of Seamus Gilfuddy: A soft, gentle and expansive face, accommodating a number of unthreatening folds of flesh. He is rarely seen without a pipe in his mouth.
*Correction: Never seen without a pipe in his mouth.
He is an accomplished cook and a lover of gourmet food. He lives alone and loves cooking dishes for himself every day, sampling culinary recipes from around the world.

Vasco was working in Dublin at the time as a Garda on the beat when Sergeant Gilfuddy 'retired' but felt he had much more to offer and would soon rise to the position of Chief Inspector once his talents were recognized. When he'd heard that the Garda station in his hometown was now unmanned, he had immediately applied for the job. The Garda headquarters in Dublin didn't really care about a tiny Garda station in a backwater and Vasco was given the job straight away despite having   only worked as a Garda for less than six months. Vasco had long desired to be a member of the Police force, mainly as a result of idolising Horatio from the television series, Miami Vice. Vasco is detached from reality and often aspires to achievements which are beyond his limited talents. It would be fair to say that he is very vulnerable to self-delusion and oblivious to his shortcomings. The truth of the matter is that, although he would not admit it, (often criticising Blarnagosha for being a backwater town) he found comfort and security there and was very happy to leave Dublin and return to his hometown. He would even have the title of Garda Sergeant and be hugely respected around the town which had not previously been the case. The words...'a bit of an eejit', has been applied to him on a few occasions by some of his fellow townsfolk.

JOCKEY TRAFFICKING IN BLARNAGOSHA

Hearing the Councilor's anguished cry, Seamus pulled up alongside in his sidecar. The sight of Seamus riding through the town in his motorcycle sidecar, with his trusty shop mannikin seated in the sidecar, dressed in a fake fur coat with her long brunette hair blowing in the wind, was familiar to all the local townsfolk but elicited bemused and bewildered stares from anyone not inured to the spectacle. Seamus had exited the local pub one night to discover that someone had placed the mannikin in the sidecar of his motorcycle while he was inside, clearly playing what they considered to be a practical joke. Seamus, however, decided to keep the mannikin housed in the sidecar, claiming that 'she' helped to provide balance as he turned sharp corners. She also provided him with 'some company' on the days he often took the sidecar for a long jaunt somewhere or other.

'Are you alright, there, Donie?'

'The bloody hell, I am'

'God, I see what you mean , was it the wind?

'There was no wind last night, only a heavy fog'

'A heavy fog|?...I didn't notice it. Mind you, nothing wakes me'.

'What?   '

'So, what caused it, d'ye think?'

'Vandals, that's what, from nearby Poolavogue. They're determined to stop us winning the tidy town again'.

'By God, that's a shame and I thought they were all quite gentle, the Poolavogue folk'

'Gentle, my arse! ... they'll bloody pay for this'

'Well, better be on my way'.

'Your mannikin's neck looks a bit crooked!'

'Ay yeah, she got a bit of a dunt from an overhanging branch when I rounded a corner a bit too sharpish...nothing that a bit of Polyfilla won't fix'

It was almost Midday when Vasco entered Peadar Scully's pub to investigate the theft of cigarettes. As it was still early in the day, the pub was almost empty of customers with the exception of a local pig farmer named Francie Joe Pilkington. However, Francie Joe was never referred to or greeted by his real name. Due to an uncanny resemblance to the Tory MP, Jacob Rees Mogg, his moniker was 'Moggy'. Resemblance, even an uncanny one, is probably an understatement. They were quite simply, doppelgangers! Mind you, any similarity to the MP ended in the replication of their physical attributes. Francie Joe rarely attended to his pig farm and spent most of his time in Peadar Scully's pub. His naturally low, mental capacity was often accentuated by the amount of alcohol he'd consumed at any given time leading often to incoherent speech patterns.

'Morning Vasc.... Sergeant.', greeted

Peadar. 'Morning Peadar.'

'I told Roisin that there was no need to call in…it was bound to be that rascal, Seamie and one or two of his friends'

'Afraid that's not how law enforcement works, Peadar.', stated Vasco pompously, as he produced a forensic dusting kit which he'd bought online with his own money as the Garda authority had refused to sanction the expense.

'You're wasting your time.'

'That remains to be seen', said Vasco. 'I take it that this is the crime scene.' he continued as he walked towards the cigarette machine.

'Yes', sighed Peadar, with an air of exhaustion

"I trust it hasn't been disturbed since the time of the crime?' Peadar chose to ignore Vasco's question.

'Gup…gwan ye….ye…' mumbled Francie Joe incoherently to himself as he raised his glass of whiskey to his lips.

'I saw your lookalike is making big news at the moment', said Vasco, turning to Francie Joe.

'Heh..him…hmm.' he muttered back

'Anyone suspicious looking been hanging around the pub recently?', Vasco asked Peadar as he began to dust ing the cigarette machine for fingerprints.

'Not that I can think of...apart from the guy with the semi-automatic machine gun who was prowling about yesterday.'

'No need for sarcasm...how about you, Francie Joe?'

'Hup...pit, pit.'

'Right, I'll be in touch.' said Vasco five minutes later after he'd completed his "forensic investigation".

'It was Seamie and his friends.' Peadar shouted as Vasco exited the pub.

'What's the story with the stolen cigarettes?' asked Roisin when Vasco entered the Garda station ten minutes later.

'Ongoing for the time being.'

Description of Roisin: She is in her early twenties. Large hazel-coloured eyes and shoulder length dark wavy hair are her outstanding features. A sharp quirky wit and a lively intelligence added to her overall allure. Sassy.

'Get up to anything last night...Vasc...Sergeant?'

'Not much, no.'

'Did you not even watch an episode of Miami Vice?' she asked playfully

'Well yeah….one or two.'

'Suppose you didn't happen to catch that David Attenborough episode about fish….it was amazing. It was about this fish, forget what it was called…anyway, it can not only change sex, but it can change sex while it's actually having sex…imagine that.'

Roisin looked to Vasco for his response and noticed that he was blushing heavily.

'Sorry, didn't mean to embarrass you.'

It was no secret around the town that Vasco had a crush on Roisin but forever denied if the subject was brought up. His discomfort was slightly relieved when Jacko, the jockey, entered the station.

'Morning to you both…. God, did either of you see that documentary on the telly last…. about that fish?' he asked, with great enthusiasm.

'I did, yeah…was just telling the Sergeant about it.'

Vasco's deep blush returned as soon as the transgendering fish was mentioned again.

'Be God, imagine changin' sex in the middle of it…I was sayin' to meself that I wouldn't know whether to put me trousers back on afterwards or her dress.'

Roisin laughed loudly as Vasco made the pretence of writing something in his notebook.

'So, you were saying earlier you wanted to talk to me about some serious matter?'

'That I do.' replied Jacko, as he climbed into a chair opposite Vasco

Jacko told Vasco that he'd heard word from a reliable source of a plan to abduct a number of jockeys from Jockeytown and traffic them to America. Apparently, there were a number of very wealthy Americans with Irish ancestry who were prepared to pay big money for an Irish jockey. Jacko had been told that once the jockey had been handed over to the buyer, he would be held captive in the basement of the house and then be shown off at intervals to the buyer's friends as a genuine leprechaun. Many Irish Americans believe that leprechauns did actually exist in Ireland over 500 years or so ago but that slowly over the years they have gradually evolved into jockeys.

'Sounds like a tall story to me, Jacko.....a tall story Blarnagosha style', Vasco said, adapting a similar sentence he'd heard Horatio from Miami Vice say on the TV the previous evening

'It's true, I'm tellin' ye...supposed to happen this weekend as well.... ignore it at your.... your.... what's the word?'

'Peril.', suggested Roisin

'Peril, thanks Roisin...peril that's the word....at your peril, Sergeant 'I'm tellin' ye...it's as true as my finger is.....is.... what's the expression, Roisin?'

'I don't know, Jacko...you have me lost on that one.'

'Anyway, forget about my finger...don't say I didn't warn ye.', were Jacko's parting words.

Description of Jacko: Small, if not tiny of stature. A large, pointed nose looks like it has been incongruously planted on his minute, wizened 'jockey' face. Speaks in a high-pitched voice which dogs can hear from a distance.

As he left, Roisin couldn't help amusing herself with the thought of a male and female jockey, with their colourful pantaloons around their ankles, engaged in lustful sexual shenanigans together and possibly changing sex at the same time.

Around the same time that Jacko was occupying Vasco in the Garda station, two middle-aged American men drove into Blarnagosha in a large camper van. They had already booked two rooms for two nights in the only B&B in Blarnagosha run by a local woman known as Mrs. B.

Description of Mrs. B: She is in her early sixties, an ill-proportioned blowsy woman, characterised in appearance by the fact that she only sports one nostril as a result of an ugly collision while playing a game of camogie in her youth. She claims that she makes the best fried breakfast in the West of Ireland, however her claim has never been put to the test (There being no authority appointed as yet to adjudicate on such matters). The walls in the dining room of

21

her B&B are bare save for a large, framed photograph of the English actress, Joanna Lumley.

Mrs. B always styles her hair in the same fashion as Joanna Lumley, and despite bearing no other resemblance to her, she was somehow convinced that she was the spitting image of her. She answered the ring on the doorbell of her B&B and opened the door to two burly men standing outside, each holding a small suitcase.

'I know what you're thinking', she said with an advancing smile on her face, 'what in the name of God in heaven is Joanna Lumley doing in Blarnagosha.'

'Eh, sorry Mam...we booked two rooms for two nights... names of Reilly and Jenson.... we got the right place?'

'Oh, of course, I should have known.... you're the Americans! '

'That's right, Ma'am.'

'Come in, come in...is Joanna Lumley well known in America?'

'Can't say she is.', replied the man named Reilly. The other man, Jenson, had yet to say anything.

'So, have you been in Blarnagosha before...you'll love it here.... oh, just one thing! you're not gay, are you?'

'Pardon me?'

'Gay…. you know like…like…is it Tom Cruise I'm thin king of?'

'Think he's a what you call it…scientologist.'

'Oh, is that what he is…'

'Anyways, in answer to your question, we're not gay.'

'That's grand so…you have to be careful these days.'

Having settled into their respective rooms, the two men stood outside the B&B fifteen minutes or so later.

'You do a recce on that side of the town.' said Reilly, pointing in a particular direction,' I'll take the other. Meet back here in a couple of hours.'

'Ok.'

CHAPTER THREE

(3 weeks earlier)

There had been rumours over the years that Francie Joe was a sexual deviant, in the manner of cavorting on occasions with one or two of his pigs. The teenager, Seamie, whom Peadar Scully suspected of the theft of cigarettes from his pub, decided one day to spy on him along with a few friends. Concealing themselves behind a few trees which bordered Francie Joe's pig sty, they sat and waited, phones ready, hoping that Francie Joe might appear and gift them a salacious video which they would post onto their social media accounts. In their minds they would just do it for a bit of fun, rather than any particular attempt to publicly humiliate Francie Joe who was probably too drunk most of the time to care that much anyway.

It happened that they were in luck that day. They were

gifted with a full five-minute video on their phones of Francie Joe engaged in an act of bestiality with one of his pigs. The video went viral after just a few hours. However, although everyone in Blarnagosha knew that it was Francie Joe in the video, the rest of the outside world saw Jacob Rees Mogg with his trousers around his ankles astride a pig. Naturally, Rees Mogg, unaware of his doppelganger in Blarnagosha, vehemently denied that it was him in the video. However, as a day or two passed it became clear that it was impossible for him to actually prove his innocence in the matter and the pressure mounted on him to retire from public life. This he did with deep reluctance on the third day of the video going viral. His denial was somewhat tempered by the previous sexual behaviour of some of his fellow Tory MPs, although he was the first one to be suspected of bestiality.

Connecticut (2 weeks earlier)

Paul Tobin is 78 years old and now retired. He had been a successful businessman for over fifty years, building up a range of businesses across the USA from cut price supermarkets, bowling alleys, nightclubs, fast food chains and even a couple of casinos in Las Vegas. In truth, he was a millionaire a few times over. He had long espoused what he referred to as his proud Irish heritage.

His great, great grandfather, Cathal Tobin, had emigrated from Ireland during the much-documented potato famine and had arrived four weeks later in New York, disembarking from a coffin ship with hundreds of other displaced Irish people, tired, penniless, and near to starvation. He was the eldest of nine brothers and five sisters who had waved to him along with his mother, Gubnit, as he had set sail from the coast of County Cork on 14th March 1843. His mother was a doughty woman, with strong features, wide shouldered to the extent that she needed to pass through doorways side on, and a pair of fists that could smash a fully grown turnip to smithereens. She had brought up all her fifteen children single-handedly as her husband, Mickey, had been a drunken layabout. She managed to keep a roof over their heads and feed them all as she was a formidable opponent in the art of bare-knuckle fighting, beating many a male opponent to a bloodied pulp in her prime.

Paul had commissioned a well-known sculptor to create a life size statue of Gubnit, which took pride of place in the expansive hallway of his mansion in Connecticut. There were no photographic records of his great, great, great grandmother but Paul had always had a vision in his head of her facial features which bizarrely resembled those of Marilyn Monroe and the sculpture was fashioned accordingly. Whenever anyone questioned why he had a sculpture of Marilyn Monroe in his hallway, he would proudly declare that it wasn't the famous actress but that it was his great, great, great grandmother, Gubnit.

It could be claimed that Paul Tobin became more and more obsessed with his long distant Irish ancestry during his advancing years. He would have his five cars painted green for one day every year on St. Patrick's Day, he would personally paint the front door of his mansion green on the same day, and wore a green suit, green shirt, and green tie when attending Mass in his local Church on St. Patrick's Day. There was a belief that he was beginning to go a bit 'soft in the head', in particular when he declared to a friend one day that he believed that leprechauns did actually exist in Ireland over 500 years ago but that gradually over the years, they had slowly evolved into jockeys.

Two well-known criminals, named Reilly and Jenson, had been instructed by an anonymous source, to meet an un-named individual in a hotel room at 3pm on the 7th of February. They were informed that it would be hugely to their advantage to attend the meeting as there was a big operation going down for which they would be paid handsomely once it had been pulled off. Both men had a record of smuggling illegal goods into the Country, usually in old ships which were often hired by them and others in parts of Eastern Europe, like Lithuania and Crimea.

They entered the hotel and made their way to the room on the third floor where they'd been instructed to go. As soon as they knocked on the door, it opened automatically. They entered a room which was in semi-darkness and could make out the shape of a man sitting behind a desk. He beckoned them forward to sit on two seats which were still about 15 or so feet away from the desk he was sitting behind. From where they were sitting, they could not make out his facial features.

A half an hour later, Reilly and Jenson were walking away from the hotel, having agreed a course of action with the mysterious man.

'What you think?', asked Jenson.

'Seems a bit off his nut, but 10 grand as a down payment ain't bad.', replied Reilly.

'Suppose, and another forty once it's done...You ever been

to Ireland before?'

'Nope, never had any reason to go there?'

'Not going to be easy taking five of them out of the Country.'

'Maybe not easy, but pretty sure it can be done...we'll use the usual shipping route.... it's just people instead of cocaine.'

''Yeah, 'cept cocaine doesn't fight back.'

'They're all old and small.... shouldn't be a problem.'

'Maybe, but we've never done it with people before... whole new ball game.'

'Trust me, it'll be okay.'

FIVE YEARS EARLIER (in Blarnagosha)

Tom Brophy had just left the house and was making his way down the short driveway when he thought he heard a feint noise behind him. He was about to turn around but never got the opportunity before someone smashed him on the back of the head with a shovel. For a split second he saw the ground coming towards him and then was consumed by darkness.

The following morning, his wife, Mrs. B, entered the Garda station to report that her husband had gone missing. The Garda Sergeant at the time was still Seamus Gilfuddy who had been in the job now for nearly 40 years. He manned the station on his own without a part-time 'PA' like his successor, Vasco Devine.

'Are you sure he's missing.... could he not have gone for a long walk, maybe.' The Sergeant suggested to Mrs. B.

'A long walk...for the whole night. He left the house at 8pm and he still hasn't returned...it's now ten in the morning, that's a very long walk.'

'Well, I suppose 'hike' would be a better word.... if my wife reported me missing every time I went for a walk through the night, be God she'd have been in the Garda station every second day of the week.', he said, trying to lighten the possible gravity of the situation.

'I'm telling you; he's missing.'

'Fair enough.... does he enjoy a smoke from a pipe?', the

Sergeant asked, slowly and meticulously filling his pipe with tobacco before lighting it.

'A pipe.... what in the name of merciful Mary, mother of virgins, has a pipe got to do with it?'

The Sergeant had enjoyed many years of near idleness while manning the local Garda station and was reluctant to break that spell.

'Maybe nothing, but I used to enjoy whiling the night away, sitting atop the ancient hill up there, puffing away contentedly on my 'ol pipe.'

'His pipe is still at home.' Mrs. B informed me, with an air of someone whose patience was about to crack.

'In that case, the matter has suddenly taken a sinister twist...I'll instigate an immediate investigation, no holes barred.'

'Thank you, I'll leave it in your hands.', Mrs. B said as she got up from her seat to leave, caressing a sliver of her hair which was clearly designed to fall down one side of her face.

A keen observer, which Sergeant Gilfuddy was most certainly not, would have noticed the upper half of a fashion magazine jutting from the top of her handbag, showing a photo of Joanna Lumley posing with an identical sliver of hair falling over one side of her face.

Vasco Devine was only twenty years old at this time. He had no particular aspiration to enter the forces of law and order at the time and worked as an assistant to his father in the butcher's shop. However, he also had no desire to follow in his father's footsteps but held much loftier plans for himself.

He couldn't decide whether he wanted to be a show business impresario (although he'd already had cards printed up advertising himself as such but had yet to put them into use.), a business entrepreneur with his finger in many pies, a famous singer,(" The Boy from Blarnagosha conquers Las Vegas." was a headline he'd often imagined emblazoned on the front page of every newspaper in Ireland) or failing that, a famous ventriloquist, as he'd been told on a few occasions that his mouth barely moved whenever he talked.

One of these ambitions was soon to be tested when Vasco learned that a crew from "Watch the Talent", a popular television show show-casing new talent every year was to arrive in Blarnagosha three weeks later to hold auditions for the show. He immediately decided to work out a ventriloquists' act for his audition. However, he soon realised that the cost of buying or commissioning a dummy was totally out of his league and he became very despondent for a couple of days. But then he hit upon an inspiration. He would ask Jacko, the jockey, to be his ventriloquists' dummy. Okay, Jacko was a real person and not a dummy, but he was tiny and actually looked a bit like a dummy. With some make up, Vasco was convinced they would get away with it. He met with Jacko later that day.

'You want me to what?', Jacko said in utter disbelief.

'It'll work, I'm telling you…I've given it a lot of thought.'

'You actually expect me to sit on your shoulder with your arm up my jockey shirt as if you were working me?'

'Exactly!'

'Exactly, my little jockeys' arse!'

'It's never been done before…no one has ever had a jockey dummy.'

'You're feckin' mad.'

'Ten quid! we could become really famous.'

'And what do I do when you're not around…. sit motionless on a chair with my legs dangling over it.'

'Twelve quid, I can't pay any more.'

'Jesus, I'm going to regret this.'

'You won't…it'll be great.'

'Do you have a script…is that what it's called?'

'Well, yeah…working on it.'

Vasco wasn't the only resident of Blarnagosha who had

decided to audition for "Watch the Talent". Mrs. B, despite the recent disappearance of her husband, had also applied. Anytime she sang a rendition of "Blanket on the ground" at a wedding, the Country song made famous by Billie Jo Spears, she'd always received a rousing reception so she decided that would be her audition piece. But not only her. Vasco's father, Gem, was going to recite some of his meat-based poetry. And there were a few other acts in the mix as well. The auditions were to be held in the old, dilapidated town hall in Blarnagosha.

The crew from "Watch the Talent " arrived in Blarnagosha a few weeks later and ensconced themselves the night before the auditions in the only hotel in the town bizarrely named "The Mozart Hotel ". The original owner of the hotel had claimed that Wolfgang Amadeus Mozart had once stayed in the establishment when it was still an old-fashioned Inn (offering rest and sustenance to the weary traveller). There was never any proof that the classical composer had spent even one night in the place, resting in his bed replete with a hearty stew inside him washed down by a local strident ale. In fact, there was absolutely nothing about the hotel to which the word 'classical' could apply. It was old and unkempt as tourists to Blarnagosha were rare in the extreme.

Vasco was aware that the crew, including the show's producer, were staying in the hotel the night before the auditions and made his way to the hotel that night to introduce himself to them and hopefully mingle with them for a while. He mistakenly thought, in his youthful naivety, that this would accord him an advantage over the other contestants. He arrived at the bar area of the hotel around 8pm that evening. The crew were the only people in the bar and were seated at a large table together. The producer, Harry Stigworth, had worked in television for many years, producing some very successful shows in his day, but due to some scandal involving a new up and coming producer, he had long since been 'demoted' to producing lesser, down market shows like "Watch the Talent". He held a deep bitterness about this and was known to have greatly increased his alcohol intake in the intervening years. He had already downed a number of whiskies by the time Vasco had arrived. Vasco immediately strode up to the table with an air of misguided, unabashed confidence.

'Vasco's the name…ventriloquism's the game.'

The crew, a total of four of them including the producer, just stared back at him without responding.

'I'm performing at the audition tomorrow, just thought I'd introduce myself.' Vasco announced, beginning to feel a slight degree of discomfort, in particular because of a steely glare from the producer. The researcher on the show, Beccy Farrell, spoke up, feeling a little sorry for Vasco.

'We don't ever meet 'the talent' before the actual auditions.'

'Or even during them, if we can avoid it.', slurred the producer as he downed another whisky.

The following night, almost the entire population of Blarnagosha and quite a few from Poolavogue, crammed into the town hall to watch the auditions. Gem, Vasco and Jacko (his ventriloquist dummy), Mrs. B, and a couple of other performers mingled about the makeshift dressing room nervously, waiting for their call to go on stage. One of the other performers, Dermot Finnehy, the manager of the local supermarket, was due to perform a magic act. He was more nervous than all the others and was trying out his magic on each of them individually. All the others tolerated him up to a point with the exception of Gem Devine who was rehearsing the first poem he was going to recite.

'No, I won't pick a card.... now feck off!'

Beccy, the researcher, popped her head around the door of the dressing room.

'Gem Devine.... five minutes please.'

'I'll be ready.'

Five minutes later, Gem Devine ambled onto the stage. The producer, Beccy and another younger guy were seated in three chairs, fronted by a table, ten yards or so from the front of the stage. Each contestant was to give their name, a very short history of who they were and the nature of their act. Once he'd done that, Gem launched into his act. He recited his first poem about the joys of a joint of lamb. The three judges were unsure when he'd come to the end of the poem and there was a short, awkward silence before they clapped with little enthusiasm, mixed with a sense of bemusement. Gem felt he would really wow them with his second poem.

> "A sirloin steak is a beatiful sight
> Not like that vegetarian shite,
> And I'll give my right arm and the
> other one too,
> for some mutton and kidneys baked in
> a stew."

Unfortunately for Gem, both Beccy and the other younger guy were vegetarians and were not impressed with Gem's second poem. The producer, Harry Stigworth, had already lost interest and was texting on his phone. Gem left the stage in complete silence, except for the sound of his shoes echoing on the creaking floorboards. Mrs. B was next up.

'Firstly, I know you're all thinking about how much I look like Joanna Lumley but please don't be distracted by that when I start to sing.'

The three judges looked utterly perplexed and weren't sure at first if she meant it as a joke. Accompanied by a karaoke backing tape, she blasted out her version of "Blanket on the ground.". She received a reasonable response, possibly helped by the fact that Gem Devine had died a death on stage and there was some relief that he was no longer there. It didn't make a great deal of difference, but Beccy was fairly sure that Mrs. B had sung the words..." Blanket underground" and not "Blanket on the ground."

MICHAEL REDMOND

The supermarket manager/magician dropped his cards in the middle of a trick and his act went to pieces after that. Then came Vasco, walking very gingerly onto the stage, balancing Jacko on his shoulder. Jacko's nose and lips were both painted with red lipstick to create the effect of a ventriloquist's dummy. Considering the poor to tepid responses which the acts before him had received, Vasco was feeling quite confident about his ventriloquist's act which he'd rehearsed almost every night up to now with Jacko atop one of his shoulders. They had rehearsed a routine based around Jacko's contention that jockeys around the world were vulnerable to large birds of prey due to the brightly coloured outfits they wore as they raced around on their horses. Vascomanaged to keep his mouth from barely moving as the dummy expressed his fears about large birds of prey. Then Vasco, as himself, would respond with his scepticism of the entire matter. The pay off at the end was the dummy proving his theory by mentioning the amount of his horses you see coming up to the finishing line without any jockeys on them. The act was actually receiving an encouraging response and the judges seemed oblivious to the fact that the 'dummy' was a real living jockey. That is, until the finale of the act when Vasco adjusted the position of his arm which was providing support for Jacko balancing on his shoulder, and Jacko fell backwards onto the stage. He'd broken his fall by putting his arm out first, but this caused him to badly sprain his wrist at the same time. Jacko jumped up screaming in agony and ran off stage.

Mrs. B came in as the only one who passed the audition, and she would go on to compete in a final to be held in

Dublin four months later.

CHAPTER FOUR

The American named Jenson was making his way down the High Street in Blarnagosha. The first shop he came to was Gem Devine's butcher's shop. He couldn't help noticing that there was a large sign on the window of the shop reading…"NO VEGETARIANS HERE. As he entered, Vasco's father and mother, Gem and Bernadette, were busy behind the counter. Bernadette was occupied with some piece of meat, trying to make it look pretty in the display cabinet. Gem was holding aloft a shank of spring lamb and eulogising about it to a bemused customer.

"With some boiled lamb on
the bone
A man is never alone
Sprinkle with some mint
Not too much, just a hint."

The customer shifted awkwardly from foot to foot as he was unsure if Gem had completed his poem and after a few seconds said...'No thanks, Gem, I'll stick with the sausages for today' and then beats a hasty retreat.

When the other customer left, Jenson approached the counter.

"Morning, wondering if you can direct me to the Jockeytown area round here?"

Gem was tending to a joint of meat with a large cleaver, so Bernadette stepped in.

"Oh, you're not too far from it at all. Mind you, they don't like us going in there."

"What's that...don't like who?"

"Well, you know people like us... of average height"

"Oh really!"

"Unless you have family there?"

"Oh, family yeah.... cousin, haven't seen him for a while"

"Oh, that'll be great for you... so, right out of the shop, second left, walk down that road for approximately 108 yards.... you can't miss it."

"Great, thanks for your help, Ma'm."

As Jenson was about to leave, Bernadette held up a string of sausages.

"Can I interest you in some sausages before you go?"

"Eh, no thanks, kinda in a hurry"

"How about some rashers of bacon for a sandwich later?...my son always has a bacon sandwich for his lunch

"Really, got to go!"

"Some boiled ham for your dinner?"

At this point, although the man Jenson was not a vegetarian, he decided his best mode of escape from the exhortations of Bernadette would be to claim that he was one.

"Actually, I'm a vegetarian."

Gem, who up to now had been busy with his meat cleaver, suddenly looked up from his task at the mention of the 'V' word. He moved out from behind the counter, walked menacingly towards the door of the shop and bolted it closed from the inside. Waving the bloodied meat cleaver in his hand, he encouraged Jenson towards a door at the back of the shop leading to a small basement area.

"No Gem, not again." pleaded Bernadette in vain

"What the goddam....", Jenson cried out as he made his way down the steps to the basement and heard the door lock behind him.

On the other side of town, Jenson's partner, Reilly, had been investigating the best possible route of escape from the town once they had executed their plan. He had decided on a small B road near the forest as it would afford good cover. He was crossing the road on his way back to the B&B to rendezvous with Jenson as arranged, when a motorcycle sidecar, driven by an elderly man, swept round a bend and he had to jump swiftly towards the pavement in order to avoid being run over by it. He couldn't have been sure, but he was almost certain that the passenger in the sidecar was a female mannikin.

CHAPTER FIVE

Later back at the Garda station, Vasco was busying himself looking at an online catalogue of sunglasses when the phone rang. Roisin picked it up. The caller was a Nun from a convent just a couple of miles outside the town. She informed Roisin that a number of young lads whom she referred to as ' skallywags' were lurking in the grounds of the convent, all smoking to their heart's content. She informed Vasco.

"Sounds like Seamie and his friend's." she suggested

"Maybe, maybe not...but time to investigate. Let's go, sounds like a two-man job.... I mean, two people.one woman and one man because that's...."

"It's alright, Sergeant...I'm sure you meant it as just an expression."

A few minutes later, they arrived at the convent in the police car. Because the town of Blarnagosha was regarded as a small remote area in policing terms, the Garda authorities didn't feel that the cost of even a standard police car could be justified. Accordingly, the car which Vasco and Roisin found themselves in was a 1986 Ford

Escort which had been donated to the local Garda station by the Blarnagosha town councilor, Donie Nesbitt. Donie had won a 'modest' amount of money on the lottery and decided to buy himself a spanking new BMW which he had always felt was the standard of car which should be accorded to a man of his stature. Rather than driving his old Ford Escort to a dump, he had donated it to the Blarnagosha Garda station in what he called a 'decent gesture of goodwill to the area.'

The nun, Sister Anastacia, who'd made the phone call to the Garda station had been called away to perform some duty or other, but Vasco and Roisin were met at the door to the convent by the Abbess, Sister Immaculata. She was a woman in her early seventies who had previously been in a Silent order of nuns but had left that order because she found it too lonesome and somewhat archaic. However, because she had been so used to living in a Silent order, she now spoke in a low, soft voice which was barely audible. When words emanated from her mouth, they sounded more like the gentle soughing of a breeze rather than spoken words. She tried her best to enunciate her words so that Vasco and Roisin would be able to understand her. However, in the end she had to resort to hand gestures to indicate that Seamie and his friends had since absconded. She pointed them in the direction of a nearby graveyard which she'd seen them skulk towards just a few minutes earlier.

Vasco and Roisin returned to their car to drive in the direction of the graveyard.

"Jesus.", Roisin sighed, as she fastened her seatbelt.

"What…what is it?' asked Vasco

"I don't know it's just…. imagine never ever having sex.'

Vasco felt the onset of a blush rising to his cheeks but tried to cover it up by stepping on the accelerator to create the mood of a police chase.

'Not even the odd shag.', she persisted.

Once again Vasco's embarrassment at the mention of sex from Roisin was relieved when he had to swerve slightly to avoid a sheep which had strayed slightly onto the road. However, he had also instinctively pressed on the car horn as a warning, forgetting that the horn was faulty and once sounded, it sometimes became stuck. Which was now the case. It would not particularly have bothered him if they hadn't rounded a corner to be met by a funeral cortege in front of them on their way to the graveyard.

The mourners in the cortege turned towards the car with looks of rage and disgust on their faces. They had naturally assumed that the driver of the car was impatiently sounding his horn for them to clear a passage for him. Vasco was trying to gesticulate to them that he wasn't deliberately sounding the horn which level of noise seemed to increase the longer it went on. He'd decided it was best to get out of the car to explain the situation to the mourners but not before two burly young men of farming stock detached themselves from the group of mourners, took a firm grip on the front of the car and between them managed to turn it sideways and left it facing the ditch on the side of the road. They then re-joined the other mourners as they all moved slowly towards the graveyard.

When Vasco and Roisin got out of the car, they noticed Seamie and a couple of his friends further up ahead on a hill but totally shielded by the mourners. They decided that any further pursuit, by passing through the mourners even on foot, could lead to further confrontation. Vasco managed after some time to turn the car round on the narrow road, horn still blaring, and they drove back in the direction of Blarnagosha.

"I could never become a nun.' continued Roisin from the conversation she was having before. Well, not so much a conversation as Vasco had not contributed anything to it.

'I don't mean just because of never having sex....
I mean, I don't even believe in God...if I did, I suppose I could go without it.'

'Do you.... em...'

'What?'

'Do you fancy going for a drink some night... doesn't have to be a date like...just....'

'Yeah, why not.'

'Oh, okay grand...', said Vasco, displaying too much

surprise that Roisin had responded positively.

'On one condition though.'

'Don't worry, doesn't have to be serious.'

'No, I don't mean that.... I mean, don't turn up wearing those sunglasses you were looking at online earlier...like the pair Horatio wears.'

CHAPTER SIX

Dusk had now set in on Blarnagosha and Reilly was becoming seriously worried. He had been supposed to meet Jenson back at the B&B over three hours ago but three was still no sign of him and his phone was just ringing out. Although they had not yet engaged in any criminality, he was reluctant to report the matter to the local Gardai. They might start questioning him about his presence in Blarnagosha and he was worried that his criminal record might somehow come to light. Very unlikely that a 'cop shop' in this distant outpost would connect him to anything but he didn't want to risk endangering the operation. But where the hell was Jenson? It had been a long day so far. They had set off from Dublin early in the morning and he had done all the driving as Jenson couldn't drive. How can anyone not goddam drive in this day and age? He'd intended to just lie on his bed for a short rest, but sleep had soon overtaken him. Reilly had thought at first that he was dreaming. Mrs. B was standing at the end of his bed, staring at him. She was speaking but he couldn't make out any words she was saying. Slowly he began to drift into wakefulness. It wasn't a dream...she was there at the end of his bed.

'Sorry to disturb you, Mr. Reilly...are you awake?'

What...what's wrong, is it Jenson?'

'Mr. Jenson...no, haven't seen him...is he missing?'

Reilly was about to say that his friend was missing but decided to keep it to himself.

'No....eh...think he's gone to meet someone, should be back soon.'

'Oh, grand, so.'

'Is there something I can do for you?'

'Oh, I was just thinking. It's almost 8 o'clock and I suspect you haven't eaten. There'll be nowhere open in the town at this time, and I have a lovely lamb casserole ready.'

Reilly was about to decline the invitation but remembered that he hadn't eaten for quite a few hours, and he could do with some food.

A few minutes later he entered the breakfast room of the B&B where he expected Mrs. B to serve him his food but there was no sign of her. She suddenly appeared at the door behind him.

'Oh, no, not in here, I've prepared a place for you in my sitting room.'

When Reilly entered the sitting room, it was dimly lit and there were a few lighted candles scared about. There was a table set with a frilly tablecloth and a small vase in the middle with a fresh rose in it. He immediately realised that he had been lured into her lair as it were, and he felt a deep sense of discomfort and alarm.

'Sit yourself down there, Mr. Reilly. Can I offer you a glass of wine...or two?'

She clearly thought that this was a hilarious thing to say and burst out laughing for a good twenty seconds or so. When she had finally exhausted her laughter buds, she placed a serving spoon into the casserole dish and poured Reilly a large glass of wine

'My husband's favourite dinner.' she said, as she spooned some of the food onto his plate.

'Thank you.', he responded, 'where's your husband tonight?'

'Oh sorry, I should have said, ex-husband...not with me anymore.'

'Sorry to hear...that's the way it goes sometimes...relationships, huh!'

Reilly swallowed a mouthful of the food which tasted surprisingly nice. Somehow, he wasn't expecting it to be.

'Well, it's not really like that...he's not with any of us anymore.... he's dead.'

Reilly was not very good at dispensing sympathy in this scenario.

'Gee.... that's...sorry about...', Reilly said after he'd swallowed a mouthful of wine and Mrs. B quickly re-filled his glass.

'Disappeared into thin air only five years ago.'...imagine that. Left the house one evening to go to the pub and never arrived there. Never seen again.'

The second mouthful of the lamb casserole began to stick in Reilly's throat. He couldn't exactly explain why but he felt that he might have trouble sleeping in the same house as the woman opposite him. There was an ineffable menace about her. However, he continued to enjoy the wine and was now on his third large glass of it.

A mile down the road, Reilly's accomplice, Jenson, shivered in the dimly lit basement of Gem Devine's butcher's shop. Within minutes of being locked down in the basement, a monitor had lit up and a video display ing different types of meat lit up the screen. There were deep insights into the different quality of cuts of meat, a short history of when humans first became carnivores and discovered the delights of eating meat, and at the end a damning indictment of all forms of vegetarianism and of the vegan culture. The video was narrated by Gem Devine who had arranged for it to be played over and over on a loop. Jenson couldn't turn the monitor off as it had been positioned high up on the wall. It was clearly intended to brainwash anyone from the perils of vegetarianism and encourage them into the culture of meat eating. Apart from the fact that he was incarcerated in a cold basement, the video was really beginning to play on his nerves. He'd already realised that there was no signal on his phone in the basement, but he took it out of his pocket once again and used the torch on it to see if there was any possible escape route from the basement.

Gem Devine had already locked up his butcher's shop for the day and he and Bernadette were back home eating dinner in their house.

'Do you not think you should go back and let him out now? I'm sure he's probably been converted by now.'

'Nah, not yet. I'll go back later.... after the pub. A few more hours down there won't do him any harm.'

'What happens when he goes to report it to Vasco?'

'Ah, don't worry about that...It's his word against

mine. Anyway, Vasco will be too busy dealing with his 'heist', Gem laughed heartily.

CHAPTER SEVEN

It had now been three weeks since Jacob Rees Mogg had been forced to resign from public life due to his unjustified association with a bestial act. However, he had since come across some information as to the real identity of the person in the video. Obviously, he already knew that it wasn't he in the video and he was determined to prove his innocence, not just to the public in general but also to his colleagues in the Tory party, some of whom had shunned him since the video had gone viral. It could be construed that some of them were not so much concerned that Rees Mogg may have sexually cavorted with a pig but that were they to come out in support of him, it could seriously damage their reputation with their constituents on whom they depended for votes. He had received an email from an undisclosed server that a pig farmer in a small town named Blarnagosha in the southwest of Ireland was the man in the video.

He knew there was a possibility that the email was some kind of prank but despite that, he felt a strong urge to pursue the possibility that he might find the identity of the man who had caused him such public disgrace and ruined his career.

He'd boarded a flight to Dublin the following day. He had since grown a respectable moustache and dispensed with his distinctive spectacles, opting to use contact lenses instead. As a result, he was not immediately recognisable. Up to now, he had been the subject of cruel taunts on occasions from members of the public who had recognised him in the street.

Rees Mogg decided to waste no time and caught a train connection from Dublin to Galway that same day. Galway was the nearest station to the area of Blarnagosha and its surrounds.

CHAPTER EIGHT

Gem Devine left Peadar Skully's pub at around 11.30 pm that evening. If his butchers' shop hadn't been on his way home, he probably wouldn't have bothered to call in and release Jenson from his incarceration in the cellar, leaving him instead to endure a full night there. Jenson wasn't sure to be more worried or relieved when he heard the key turning in the lock of the cellar door. Thoughts went through his mind that this maniacal butcher was merely biding his time till night fell to come back and butcher him with his cleaver.

The door screeched open, and Gem Devine shone a torch down into the cellar

"You can come out now", he said, without any encouragement or hint of sympathy.

Jenson walked gingerly up the steps of the cellar. Because the torch was shining directly at him, he couldn't make out if the butcher was still holding his meat cleaver. When he reached the top of the stairs, the butcher moved

back into the shop to allow him to egress from the dimly

lit cellar. It took Jenson a few moments to adjust his eyes to the full light upstairs in the shop.

'I hope you've learned a few things from this', Gem said, with some threat in his voice.

If he'd still been holding the meat cleaver, Jenson would undoubtedly have played along and agreed that he had indeed learned a lesson. However, the butcher was not only not holding the meat cleaver but was swaying slightly on his feet and there was a strong smell of alcohol on his breath.

'You're a goddamn lunatic, you know that!', Jenson barked

'Who the hell are you call....'

However, Gem Devine was unable to finish his sentence before Jenson's fist smashed into his face and he fell to the floor, holding his bloodied nose. Jenson stormed out of the shop, leaving Gem to tend to his wounded nose and his even more damaged pride. It was a very dark moonless night, and it took Jenson quite a few moments to get his bearings and find the route back to the B&B. On the route he was surprised to see a tractor being driven down the main street at full speed and then making its way out of the town.

Gem Devine slowly lifted himself back onto his feet, cursing softly to himself.

'Fucks' sake...never known a vegetarian to pack a punch like that.

He stumbled out of his butcher's shop, locking it behind him, and walked the short distance home. Bernadette had already gone to bed but was awoken by the sound of a table lamp crashing to the floor after Gem had walked into it in the sitting room. She made her way downstairs, still unsure if there maybe was an intruder in the house. Gem had since turned the main light on in the sitting room and was sitting in an armchair when Bernadette gingerly peeped her head around the door from the safety of the hallway. She immediately spotted Gems' bloodied nose.

'Gem, what happened to you.... did you take a fall?'

'You could bloody say that...that feckin' vegetarian whacked me in the face.'

'Well, can you really blame him...locking the poor man up like that.'

'Jesus, not only is half the world becoming vegetarians, but they're becoming violent as well.'

'Hmmm.... anyway, speaking about that, I have something important to tell you.'

'Oh, what's that?'

'You're not going to like it, Gem.'

At the same time, Vasco and Roisin were arriving outside the house. They'd gone out drinking together after work

MICHAEL REDMOND

but not to Peadar Skully's pub. There was a slightly more modern pub a mile or so further up the road where the clientele tended to be younger.

'I thought you said you had your own flat.', Roisin said when they arrived outside Vasco's parents' house.

'Well, I do, more or less...I have my own entrance.'

'What do you mean?'

'You just climb up the ladder directly into my room...self-contained.'

'Is this a joke?'

'No, it's like my parents are flat mates...we just share the kitchen and bathroom.'

'You're asking me to climb up that ladder into your bedroom when there's a door just there.'

Vasco was about to respond when they were both disturbed by loud shouting from inside the house. They couldn't hear what was being said but it was clear that an argument was in full swing.

'You've become a what?', Gem shouted at his wife, 'A feckin' vegan....me own wife.....a vegan.....sufferin' fuckin' Jaysus, have you lost your mind' Gem demanded to know.

Bernadette remained sitting in her chair, an expression of calm on her face.

'What the.... what the hell am I going to tell people.... I'll be a bloody laughingstock! a butcher with a vegan wife.'

'Probably not the first time it's happened.' Bernadette suggested, but a bit too lamely.

'NOT THE FIRST TIME!...NOT THE FIRST TIME!.... of course, it's the bloody first time.'

Silence then ensued.

'I wonder what the hell that was all about?',

'Sounded serious alright!'

'I think I heard my father say something like... not the first time it's happened.... Jesus, do you think he's having an affair?

'Hardly.... I wouldn't jump to conclusions. Anyway, what the hell, Vasco...let's get up that ladder.' Roisin said with a glint in her eye.

CHAPTER NINE

The town of Poolavogue was a mere five miles inland from Blarnagosha and both towns had lived in harmony with each other for many years. However, a degree of tension had begun to break out in recent years as a result of Blarnagosha pipping Poolavogue to the winning post in the West of Ireland tidy town competition for two years in a row. A six-foot-high statue of its most noteworthy citizen, Kevin Cartwright, stood proudly at the top of the main street. Kevin Cartwright had emigrated to America in the latter part of the nineteenth century and was celebrated for becoming a captain of industry only six years later in the so-called 'land of the free', despite arriving in the country almost penniless.

Donie Griffin arrived in Poolavogue around 12.20 am, twenty minutes after tearing out of Blarnagosha in his borrowed tractor. He was very aware of how much significance the statue of Kevin Cartwright accorded to the town. Seemingly oblivious to the possibility of personal injury, he pointed the tractor in the direction of the statue, picking up as much speed as possible as he went, ramming the back of the statue, which swayed back and forth for a few seconds before toppling to the ground. Donie managed to emerge from the collision with only a minor injury, a slight sprain to his right wrist. He turned the tractor back in the direction of Blarnagosha, punching the air triumphantly as he went and laughing in a loud, maniacal voice.

When Jenson arrived back at the B&B around the same time as Donie Griffin had dismantled the statue in Poolavogue, the house was in total darkness. He cursed quietly to himself, remembering that Reilly had the only key which Mrs. B had given them earlier. Jenson took out his phone and phoned Reilly. Not only was Reilly already immersed in a deep sleep in his bed but had forgotten to charge his phone beforehand which was now laying on his bedside table, dead to the world. He was going to ring the front doorbell but decided instead to go round the back of the house to see if the back door might be open. He was in luck. He quickly made his way up to Reilly's room and entered without knocking. He heard a slight stirring in the bed and turned on the light. It took him a few seconds that the woman in bed with Reilly was Mrs. B, the owner of the B&B.

Mrs. B was the first to react.

'Oh, merciful heaven.' she gasped

She jumped out of the bed, half naked and grabbed the rest of her clothes which were lying on the floor beside the bed.

'God knows what state my hair must be in.', she wailed, as she ran out of the room.

Reilly rubbed his bleary looking eyes to adjust to the sudden light. He couldn't remember finishing the third bottle of wine or how the landlady had ended up in bed with him.

'Where the goddamn hell have you been?', he asked

'Not having as good a time as you by the looks of it.', said Jenson with a scowl on his face.'

'What happened.... why didn't you meet back here as arranged?'

'You won't fucking believe it! ,spent the last seven hours locked in the basement of the local butcher's shop.'

'You what?'

'Goddamn bloody lunatic he is.... thought I was a vegetarian and locked me in his cellar with some crazy video on a continuous loop.'

' What...what kind of video?'

'Some fucking video he's made up about the joys of eating meat.... anyway, doesn't matter now.'

Reilly couldn't prevent himself from laughing.

'Yeah, real fucking funny it is.'

'Sorry, buddy....You have any luck locating Jockeytown? ...seems I was on the wrong side of town for it.'

'Yeah, know where it is.... I'm going to bed, need some sleep real bad.'

'Okay, we'll do a recce around Jockey Town tomorrow.'

CHAPTER TEN

(Day 2)

20th February 2028

Rees Mogg boarded the train to Galway from Houston station in Dublin at 10.am en route to Blarnagosha. No one seemed to take any notice of him apart from a middle-aged couple who were seated just two seats away. The man in particular kept staring over at him. Rees Mogg began to stir uneasily in his seat, assuming that the man had seen through his disguise. His discomfiture became more acute when only 15 minutes into the journey, the couple got up from the seats they were in and began to move towards him.

'God almighty, I was just saying to the wife.... aren't you the spitting image of your man, Lord Lucan...if this was twenty-five years ago, I'd have bet me life savings on it that you were him.'

Before Rees Mogg had a chance to respond, the man and his wife plonked themselves down on the seats opposite him.

'You don't mind if we sit with you.', the man said without any clear intention of waiting for an answer from Rees Mogg.

'Image of him, you are...spittin' image.' the woman who was being referred to as, "the wife", declared in a manner not supportive of any counter argument to her statement...'first thing I said to Jimmy when I saw you, wasn't it, Jimmy?'

'It was..when the wife says it, I looks over and Jaysus, I said to myself, she's right...Lord feckin' Lucan.',

The beleaguered Rees Mogg wasn't sure how to respond to these overtures from Jimmy and 'the wife'.

'Yes, I suppose there's a resemblance.' was what he came up with.

'Your voice is very familiar...do I know you at all?', asked Jimmy.

'I don't think that's likely, no.'

'Are you sure?...definitely heard that voice somewhere before.'
'Sure leave the poor man alone, Jimmy...if he knew you, wouldn't he have said so.'

At this point, 'the wife' began rustling inside a large plastic supermarket bag and produced a mound of sandwiches wrapped in swathes of tin foil. She ceremoniously placed the sandwiches on the table in front of them and peeled off the upper half of the tin foil, with the delicacy and deep rooted concentration of someone dismantling a bomb.

'Can I interest you in a cheese sandwich?', she said, pushing the now exposed crudely made sandwiches towards Rees Mogg.

'Oh, no...thank you very much all the same.'

'You'd be mad not to take one...the wife makes a great cheese sandwich.'

'Yes, I'm sure, but I breakfasted already.... very kind of you to offer'

'Jaysus, I've got it now.... I knew you sounded familiar.... that Rees Mogg fella.....always wears glasses and.....'

Jimmy moved forward in his seat to get an even closer look at the contours of Rees Mogg's face.

'It...it is you, isn't it. Can't blame you trying to disguise yourself after all that business with the.... was it a pig?'

'I can assure you; it wasn't me...just someone who had a very close resemblance to me.'

'But it is you...here I mean. Can't believe the wife and meself are sitting opposite Jacob Rees Mogg.... the lord between us and all harm...should I call you, Jacob.... or what?'

'Yes, Jacob will do fine.'

'Jimmy Corcoran, and this is the wife.'

'How do you do.... I wonder could I ask you both to keep who I am quiet...I'm travelling incognito.'

'Oh, don't worry.... not a word.' the wife reassured him, 'are you sure you won't have a cheese sandwich?'

'No really...no thank you.'

Thankfully for Rees Mogg, the couple lapsed into a verbal silence for ten minutes or so as they munched very noisily on the cheese sandwiches.

Meanwhile in Blarnagosha, the former Sergeant, Seamus Gilfuddy, pulled up on his motorcycle sidecar, with his trusty mannikin in tow, outside Gem Devine's butcher's shop. He always treated himself on a Saturday to a lamb roast.

'Morning Gem.'

'Seamus', Gem greeted back but in a somewhat detached voice.

'You don't seem yourself day, Gem...
something up?'

'You could say that.... it's Bernadette,'

'Oh dear...what's happened, is she ill?'

'Well, ill as far as I'm concerned.... she doesn't seem to think so. To tell you the truth, I still can't believe it.'

'God, Gem, what is it...believe what?'

'She's become a bloody vegan, that's what.'

'A vegan, by God.... becoming very popular these days. Is that why she's not in the shop today?'

'I fired her that's why.... what would it look like.... a vegan working in my butcher's.'

'That's a terrible shame altogether.'

'Apparently it's not even grounds for divorce if your wife becomes vegan.'

The former Sergeant pondered this for a moment.

'No, I don't think a change of diet would be grounds for divorce.'

Gem just muttered to himself as he prepared and packaged the joint of lamb for the former Sergeant who thanked him and made to leave. He was going to offer some word of support to Gem but decided against it as he'd already disappeared into the back of the shop, and he could hear the sound of a meat cleaver being brought down repeatedly with force on a butcher's table.

Not long after consuming some of her own homemade cheese sandwiches, 'the wife' fell into a deep sleep in her seat. Jacob Rees Mogg couldn't help noticing that a small crumb of bread had become glued to the corner of her mouth, along with a tiny ball of cheese which seemed to act as a kind of adhesive to prevent the crumb falling away. He also noticed that each time a breath escaped from her mouth that the offensive crumb fluttered enticingly with a false promise of flight away from her mouth. Her husband, Jimmy, however, was still very wide awake and keen to engage Rees Mogg in conversation.

'Tell me, this.... your man, Johnson. Is he a complete chancer altogether?'

'Well, I don't....

'Don't worry, just between you and me...won't go any further than here.... you have me word on that.'

'People have the wrong impression of Boris... deep down he's actually very shy and retiring and is very fond of knitting.'

'You're having me on?'

'No, it's quite true. There were times when I've had important meetings with him in his room in number 10 as he skilfully skipped from one stitch to the next while discussing world affairs and so on at the same time.'

'Ah go on now, you're pullin' me leg.'

'Not at all.'

'What about your man, Rishi Sunak?'

'He is an alien.' Rees Mogg replied without any hint of irony.

Rees Mogg was hugely relieved to see the small ball of breadcrumb and cheese detach itself from the corner of 'the wife's' mouth, fly erratically in the air for a split second or so before finding a home for itself on the table in front of them.

CHAPTER ELEVEN

The townsfolk of Poolavogue were enraged when they woke up that morning to discover the statue of their revered citizen had been toppled to the ground in an act of willful violence. An emergency meeting was called for that afternoon at 2pm by the town councillor, P.J.O'Herlihy, in the town hall to discuss the gravity of the situation and how to respond to this act of aggression from what he called, ' the enemies of Poolavogue.' A number of suggestions were considered but one in particular was finally settled on. There was one dissenting voice who felt the plan was fraught with danger, even possible danger to life, but the large majority won through, and the vote was carried.

You couldn't really say that there was an actual border between Blarnagosha and Poolavogue but there was an area of about 150 yards or so which had been in dispute in the past, in particular going back to the 4th century and the time of St. Patrick. Back then there was a strategic hill which divided the two communties. In order to enter Blarnagosha from Poolavogue, you had to surmount the hill. Parts of the hill still remained but a steep ascending road now ran through it from

Poolavogue to Blarnagosha. Up to now, no one really cared about the previously disputed 150 yards as it had long since lost any real significance.

That morning, Roisin had been in conversation with her father, Jerome, who owned and ran the local caravan park named, 'Paradise Park'. It has to be said that there was very little about the caravan park to suggest that anyone within its confines could enjoy the pleasures of living in Paradise. Ever since his wife had run off with a travelling street juggler from Guatemala 10 years before, Jerome had let the park fall into near rack and ruin and as it stood, there were only about three caravans left that were actually habitable. At breakfast, Roisin had just happened to mention to him in passing about Jacko's contention that there was a plot to traffic jockeys from Blarnagosha to America. She had mentioned it in a slightly playful way but there was a small part of her that felt there just might be some truth in it. She knew that Jacko was given to fantasy at times but there was something about the way he brought the matter up with Vasco that belied his customary line of nonsense.

'Well now, that's very interesting you should say that.', Jerome said, with an air of conspiracy in his expression.

'Why…what do you mean, Dad?'

Jerome went on to tell Roisin about a couple who had arrived the day before in what he described as a 'suspiciously windowless van.' He also mentioned that they both wore sunglasses throughout the entire time in his small office when he was taking their details and said they hardly spoke except when necessary and seemed very on edge. Roisin decided to mention her father's story to Vasco when she arrived at work this following morning. It would also provide something immediate to talk about to Vasco so neither of them would have to address the events of the previous night when she'd spent a few hours in Vasco's bedroom, something she was regretting already. She still wasn't convinced there was any substance to either Jacko's warning of an impending jockey trafficking operation or to her father's suspicions about the couple staying in his caravan park, but apart from mundane paperwork, there was nothing else to occupy the forces of law and order in Blarnagosha that morning. Vasco had admitted that the fingerprint samples which he'd taken from the cigarette machine in the pub couldn't be matched to any fingerprints on file as the 'forensic package' which he'd bought online was seriously flawed and insufficient for his purpose. He would just have to wait until some evidence cropped up about the culprit. Maybe someone might notice someone else smoking more than their usual amount of cigarettes and report the matter to him sooner rather than later. Vasco agreed with Roisin that the couple in the caravan park just might be worth investigating.

'At the end of the day, if we don't hang together, we die alone.', Vasco said cryptically, repeating a phrase which Horatio from Miami Vice had once said.

Roisin was about to question the significance of Vasco's statement in reference to the task they were about to undertake but thought better of it. They jumped into the old Ford Escort together and headed towards Paradise Park.

Roisin had told her father to possibly expect a visit from them in the morning, so he wasn't particularly surprised when he saw them pulling up outside his office in the Ford Escort. He was a stickler for conducting any business inside his office, no matter how trivial. He had once arrived outside his office one morning at the same time as the postman but still insisted that the postman enter his office in order to hand him over his post. He'd ignored the fact that the postman had uttered the word, "Gobshite", on his way out. Accordingly, he didn't leave his office to greet them but waited for them to enter. He was in the process of polishing a pair of his shoes, of which he owned two pairs, and polished both meticulously every day.

'Be with you in a moment.' he said, without looking up, as he swept the brush in a flamboyant manner across the toe of one of the shoes.

'Right, that should do that till tomorrow.... afraid you've missed them. I saw them leave about 15 minutes ago.'

'Think they've gone for good?' asked Vasco

'Doubt it, they're booked in for another night and they've paid for it. There's probably nothing to this...they just seemed a bit suspicious.'

'Sometimes nothing can turn into something and something into nothing if you're not looking in the right place for.... something.'

'What do you mean?' asked Jerome

'Never mind, Dad...anyway, can we have a look at the

caravan?'

Jerome led them down the dusty interior path/road to the couples' caravan. Vasco and Roisin tried to peek inside, but the tattered curtains were pulled over and they couldn't make out anything inside. Jerome produced a key from his pocket.

'Want you have a look inside?', he said, with a sly smile on his face and jangling the keys enticingly in front of Vasco.

'Don't think that's legal, Jerome.' Vasco replied, 'we'd need a warrant.'

'Be legal for me though as the owner of the place.'

Vasco didn't object to Jerome's suggestion. Jerome placed the key in the door and opened it widely so that Vasco and Roisin could see inside. He didn't have to look very far. On the table in front of him were cuttings from horse racing magazines about upcoming events in the horse racing schedule. There was also an opened almanac of jockeys, past and present, with their photographs and history of their achievements on horseback. Jerome picked them all up and returned to the door to show them to Vasco and Roisin.

'Maybe that jockey fella knows what he's talking about.' Jerome said, tapping the documents with his free hand.

'Yep, stick around, police work is full of surprises.'

Vasco didn't see Roisin raising her eyes heavenwards when

he quoted Horatio for the second time that day.

'Now we play the waiting game and return tomorrow' Vasco announced and let Jerome lead them back to his office as he'd re-locked the door of the caravan.

Roisin hadn't yet spoken to Vasco about their somewhat drunken misadventure in his bedroom the night before. 'Yes, that's what it was...a misadventure', she thought to herself.

432 AD

Patrick stood at the bottom of the hill looking up to Blarnagosha from Poolavogue. He had gathered a force of over 200 men, all armed with an early prototype of the crossbow. Despite the fact that his life has been chronicled many times, very few people are aware that Patrick's main goal in Ireland was not to convert the pagan Irish to Christianity (for which he was later granted the status of sainthood by the Vatican) but to create a culture of freedom of sexual expression. This quest stemmed from the fact he suffered enormous emotional trauma from taunts he'd received as a teenager when he'd bravely come out as being gay at the tender age of fifteen. Forced out of his home by his parents when he was only 16 years old, Patrick sought refuge in Ireland and managed to secure passage on a boat leaving Wales the following day. None of the 200 men he had gathered claimed to be gay but were mercenaries paid by Patrick to attack and defeat the Pagan tribe in Blarnagosha who were known at the time to throw anyone they suspected of being gay over the nearest cliff.

Following three days of fierce fighting, Patrick and his forces overcame the resistance of the Pagan tribe and liberated the town of Blarnagosha from sexual repression.

Once the Catholic Church had established itself in Ireland

200 years later, they re-invented Patrick as the man who'd converted the Pagan Irish to Christianity.

A force of over 500 missionaries had been sent from the Vatican to infiltrate Irish tribes and force them into Christian beliefs. They were reports of cruel torture and sometimes death to anyone who didn't succumb. The Vatican decided to cover up all these atrocities, credited Patrick for converting the Irish to Christianity and then made it official by granting him a sainthood. St. Patrick has also never been credited (if credited is the word) with introducing the rule that Catholics were denied the right to eat meat on Fridays as a sort of penance. Since that time and even up to recently when the Catholic Church still exerted a huge influence on the Country, all Catholics in Ireland felt compelled to avoid eating meat on Fridays and fish became the mainstay meal of most households on Fridays. Fortunately, since the 1980's the influence of the Catholic Church began to wane considerably and now just a tiny minority observe the rule.

However, for many years the 'fish on Fridays' rule was strictly observed. There was fish everywhere in Ireland on Fridays, the entire Country stank of fish, so much so that seagulls would fly in from abroad just for the day. There were people wandering about

with herrings sticking out of their coat pockets as they went on their way home, streets strewn with half dead lobsters trying to make a run for it. Occasionally, Protestants living in the Country whose religion exempted them from the rule, were occasionally mugged by gangs of recalcitrant Catholics if it was thought they might be carrying a sausage roll on them.

St. Patrick also invented an early version of Guinness, and the formula was later to be stolen by the Guinness family in the 19th Century.

He was also the first man to fashion a hurley stick, start a local Gaelic football league, and allow priests from the Catholic Church to take young boys away on holidays.

However, he could also be somewhat of a demagogue when the mood suited him. He was strictly opposed to any form of vegetarianism to the extent of creating a culture whereby vegetarians became ostracised from society and many of them were sent to England to avoid bringing shame on their families. In fact, even to this day, there is more of a taboo about being vegetarian than there is about being gay. For example, gay marriage is now legal in Ireland (a cause close to St. Patrick's heart) but vegetarians are still not allowed to marry each other in Ireland.

MICHAEL REDMOND

Excerpts from the diary of St. Patrick

It appears that Patrick decided to keep a diary at some point. Records of it were found when his grave was accidentally stumbled upon recently. It seems that he only persisted with it for a week or so and he only mentions the day, not the date.

MONDAY

I came across the woman, Kathleen Ni Houlihan, today on my way to chair a meeting of a small group of transvestites who are suffering verbal and on one occasion physical abuse from a breakaway group of Pagans who still don't accept me as the Saviour of the land. Anyway, to cut a long story short as my old uncle Albert used to say, Kathleen was born without any arms. She is a very expressive woman both verbally and physically but since she cannot gesticulate with her arms like everyone else, she tends to gesticulate with her legs instead. Many people in the town found this very unsettling and after a while it was decided that she was probably a witch. So, one day she was taken by some of the townsfolk to the nearby river and thrown in to see if she would sink. But she didn't sink and kept herself afloat by kicking her legs about like nobody's business. She was swept downstream still kicking her legs about like there was no tomorrow. She survived the ordeal and has since invented a type of dance in which only the legs are seen in action.

Other people with arms are beginning to ape her by keeping their arms down by their side and just kicking their legs up and down. I can't help wondering if this form of dancing will become totally unique to this island and be referred to simply as "Irish Dancing."

FOOTNOTE:

It is believed Michael Flatley has seen a copy of Patrick's diary and inspired by Kathleen Ni Houlihans' 'dance' on the river, he came up with the name of 'Riverdance' for his spectacle of Irish dance.

TUESDAY

I've introduced a vegetable called 'the potato' to Ireland. It is very popular in Wales from where I originate. A few Irish people have tasted it on my recommendation, but it doesn't seem to be to their taste, so I don't think it's going to take off here.

WEDNESDAY

My boyfriend, Denis, suggested today that we move in together. I'm not sure about this as I like having my own space and I just know he's going to want to change the decor of the bathroom. I love my pastel shades and he prefers his bold colours.

THURSDAY

A group of Pagans' who were performing some cultish ritual in the woods this evening called me 'a hairy gobshite' as I was passing by minding my own business. There's no need for that!

FRIDAY

I had a visit from Dono and his friend, The Hedge today. His friend is called 'The Hedge' because of the style and texture of his hair. It grows wildly in all directions and its tufts resemble small twigs you find on hedges. I don't know why 'Dono' is named as such because his real name is Ronnie. They are both musicians. Dono sings and The Hedge plays the lute. He's very good at it and Dono isn't a bad singer but nothing like as good as he thinks he is. They want to do a benefit concert for the minority of ginger haired people in Ireland who are discriminated against merely because of their colouring. Also, parents of ginger children are forbidden to name their children.... they are either called, 'ginger boy' or 'ginger girl'. He means well, does Dono, but he can be a bit of a pain in the arse. Anyway, I told him he has my support. The Hedge usually just smiles and nods and Dono does all the talking. Mind you, it would be hard for The Hedge to get a word in edgeways when Dono is in full voice.

SATURDAY

There's a guy works down the fish stall thinks he's Jesus. Poor lad is deluded.

SUNDAY

Dono and The Hedge have written a couple of songs for the benefit concert in aid of the ginger minority. The first song is clearly a reference to the prevailing culture in Ireland at the moment and is called..." Where the gingers have no name." The other song is called, "I still haven't found what I'm looking for.". I think it's a reference to Dono's ongoing search to find a grip on his polevault that suits him best.

It is not known if Patrick just stopped writing up a diary at this point or if pages have been lost but there are no further entries.

CHAPTER TWELVE

Although the previously disputed area of 150 yards div
iding Blarnagosha and Poolavogue dating back to the
time of St. Patrick was really irrelevant today, it was
still not strictly either in the boundary of Blarnagosha or
Poolavogue.

Geographically it was known as no mans' land as the road
sign welcoming you into Blarnagosha was a distance of 150
yards from the sign in the other direction welcoming you
into Poolavogue. Remarkably, one of the crossbows used by
St. Patrick and his 'sexually liberal' forces in the 4th century
still survived to this day and was kept in a secured glass
fronted case in a room off the main area of the town hall. P J
Herlihy and a couple of other locals from Poolavogue stood
beside the sign welcoming you into Poolavogue. One of the
men, simply known as Benjy, had once competed in a local
archery competition and had won it. He held the ancient
crossbow in his hand pointed towards the "Welcome to
Blarnagosha" sign but the crossbow was so heavy, it needed
to be supported by the other man with his arms, kneeling
on the ground in front of Benjy

.

'Are you sure about this?' Benjy asked PJ

'Course I am…it'll teach them a lesson.'

'Right you be.'

The idea was to severely puncture the "Welcome to Blarnagosha" sign, defacing the words and even hopefully toppling the entire sign. However, as Benjy was about to release the arrow from the crossbow, the man balancing the bow from below slipped and the arrow flew out from the bow in a crooked trajectory and missing the intended target by over ten yards. At the same time, Seamus Gilfuddy was riding his motorcycle sidecar, with his trusty mannikin ensconced beside him, along the road from Blarnagosha to Poolavogue. P J Herlihy gasped loudly as he looked on in horror as the arrow looked to be heading directly for him. Fortunately, Gilfuddy had reached a slight bend in the road and Seamus was oblivious of the arrow which flew just past him but lodged in the head of his mannikin, beheading her immediately. The mannikin's head lay crudely on the side of the road with the arrow still lodged in it where her nose had once been.

CHAPTER THIRTEEN

(3 years earlier in Blarnagosha)

Although Vasco had not made any further attempts at a career in ventriloquism, he still felt smitten by what he called 'the showbiz buzz'. He found himself getting excited by even mentioning the words, 'Showbusiness Impresario' and he knew that that must be where his future lay. It certainly didn't lie in working for years in his father's butcher's shop and then eventually taking it over once his father retired.

If Vasco had believed in astrology, he would have felt that on this day, 21st October 2021, his stars were in total alignment. He'd first read in the local newspaper that Kylie Minogue was performing for two nights in a large venue in Dublin four weeks from then. He'd almost missed an important piece of information at the end of the newspaper piece informing the reader that Kylie Minogue had ancestral roots in the west of
Ireland and has always held a special place in her heart for the area. He couldn't afford a ticket to see the show but that didn't stop him heading to Dublin on the bus four weeks later. He booked in for a night in some dingy B&B not far

from the city centre and later made his way to the venue where Kylie Minogue was performing. He knew he couldn't get in to see the show, but he hung around outside the stage door entrance hoping to catch her on her way out after the show.

There were quite a few other people waiting outside as well hoping to either get a selfie with the Australian songstress or just to even see her up close. However, after waiting an hour or so, most of them began to drift away. Two hours later, Vasco was the only one still waiting outside the stage door. Vasco's heart skipped a beat or two when a limousine pulled up outside the stage door and Kylie Minogue suddenly emerged fromthe building and he found himself standing only inches from here. He knew that this was his chance.

'Em...Kylie...Miss Minogue'. he spluttered awkwardly.

'Hi', she greeted with a friendly smile, 'you wanting a selfie?'

'Oh, yeah but I was wondering something else...if..'

'Okay, as long as it's not a marriage proposal.', she smiled playfully.

'No, no, its.... I'm a Showbiz Impresario and was wondering if you'd like to do a special show in the West of Ireland, a place called Blarnagosha...because, you know, of your roots and all that?'

'Oh, you'd have to talk to my Agent about that.... anyway,

have to rush.'

Before Vasco had time to respond, she'd already jumped into the limousine which sped off very quickly. When Vasco returned to Blarnagosha the next day, he could seen removing the posters which he'd plastered about the place which read.... COMING TO BLARNAGOSHA VERY SOON... THE ONE AND ONLY KYLIE MINOGUE!!!!
He tolerated the ridicule he'd received from locals for a couple of weeks following his short and unsuccessful foray into the world of show business promotion. He took a train to Dublin one Monday morning, vowing never to return to Blarnagosha. A few weeks after arriving in Dublin, he received a letter from his mother telling him he'd been accepted into the Police Force. Vasco had almost forgotten that he'd applied in the first place but not long after that he found himself working as a 'cop on the beat' on the streets of Dublin.

CHAPTER
FOURTEEN

When Reilly and Jenson arrived down for breakfast in the B&B the following morning, there was an elderly priest sitting at a table in the corner on his own. He didn't look up from his breakfast when they arrived into the room and when Reilly bade him a good morning, he barely acknowledged the greeting with a very slight nod of his head. Mrs. B came blustering into the room from the kitchen a few seconds later, carrying two plates with fried breakfasts on them. She was still feeling mortified about the events of the previous night and found it impossible to meet Reilly's or Jenson's eyes as she placed their breakfasts on the table. However, she did feel obliged to mention the presence of the priest in the corner.

'That's Father Tumelty, the former Parish priest of the area. He's a permanent guest here since he...retired.', she whispered to them while still averting her eyes from them, 'likes to keep himself to himself.'

Jenson couldn't help but notice that Reilly received an extra sausage and slice of bacon on his plate compared to his.

Father Tumelty had been in permanent residence at Mrs. B's for over three years. It was claimed that he had retired but the truth was that the Catholic Church had removed him from his post due to his excessive drinking. This had culminated one Sunday morning while he was conducting Mass. During his sermon, he was heard to be slurring his words and at one point abandoned the theme of the sermon altogether and began dispensing horse racing tips for a meeting at Galway racecourse the following day, much to the confusion of the congregation gathered before him. However, Father Tumelty's descent into the mire of alcohol addiction was not merely by chance. He had been keeping a dark secret inside him for a few years and it had begun to eat away at him. His only escape from it was through alcohol but even alcohol couldn't totally dull the demons which haunted him every day. He had heard a confession from a local person in Blarnagosha admitting to a murder but because of the sanctity of the confessional he could not reveal the identity of the person to the authorities.

However, once he had been relieved of his duties, he had approached the person who had confessed to the murder and mentioned that he was now going to reveal the terrible secret he had been keeping inside him until now.
But following a conversation with the murderer, he had agreed to hold back from exposing the grisly business in return for certain favours which would accrue to him.

Description of Father Tumelty: Stern of face with

uncompromising red blotches on both cheeks. Two abundant clumps of nasal hair have been allowed to grow unchecked from each nostril.

CHAPTER FIFTEEN

Jacob Rees Mogg arrived in Blarnagosha around 5pm that day in a taxi. Ever since the closure of the Mozart Hotel a couple of years earlier, the only establishment providing accommodation in Blarnagoasha was Mrs. B's B&B. As the taxi was arriving in Blarnagosha, Rees Mogg thought he'd noticed a disturbing sight on the grass verge lining the road and asked the taxi driver to stop. Walking back along the grass verge, the sight he came upon was indeed disturbing but not as devastating as he'd first thought. It took him a few seconds to recognize that the head in which the arrow had embedded itself was not human but that of a mannikin. The taxi dropped him a couple of minutes later outside Mrs. B's B&B. As Rees Mogg exited the taxi, the taxi driver called after him…" Can't wait to tell everyone that I had the nephew of Lord Lucan in my taxi." Rees Mogg smiled wryly at the fact that the taxi driver had believed him when he'd told him Lord Lucan was his uncle. The door to the B&B was opened as ever by Mrs. B.

'Good evening, good lady, I was wondering if you have any vacancies?'

'Francie Joe! how dare you turn up on my doorstep, ye

filthy, depraved blackguard ye'

'I'm sorry, Madam, I think you may have mistaken me for someone else.'

'God almighty, you don't sound like him to be fair.....but you're the spittin' image.'

'Hmmm, that seems to be happening to me rather a lot in the last couple of days.'

'Anyway, I'm afraid you're out of luck. I only have two rooms, and each is already occupied by two American gentlemen.'

'Oh, I see, that's unfortunate.... can you recommend anywhere else?'

'Well, I'm afraid that I'm the only recognised B&B in the area, but I do know that since Jacko the jockey's mother died, he has a spare room.... what height are you?'

'Height?'

'Yes, what height are you?'

'Well, I'm six feet, two...why do you...?'

'Well, the houses in Jockeytown are quite small to facilitate the jockeys.... are you good at bending?'

'I expect I could.... look, is this some kind of joke?'

'Good God, no...I wouldn't send you on a wild goose chase.'

'There's actually an area here called, Jockeytown?'

'Yes, straight back up the road, turn left and it's on your right after about 100 yards.'

'Good, well, thank you.' Rees Mogg said as he turned to leave, still unsure whether or not the woman was mad or playing a joke on him.

'Tell Jacko that Mrs. B sent you...or if you like, Joanna Lumley.', she shouted after him.

"Joanna Lumley", Rees Mogg mused to himself. The woman was clearly insane, but he had nothing to lose by following her directions. His mood was lifted by the fact that she had completely mistaken him for a local who must have been responsible for the obscene act with a pig. He knew now that he was in the right place if he was ever going to clear his damaged name and reputation.

When the former Garda Sergeant Seamus Gilfuddy pulled up outside his house later, he did notice that his mannikin's head was missing. In fact, it looked like it had been torn off with some violence. This sight completely puzzled him as he knew that the mannikin had been intact when he'd set off earlier for a jaunt on his motorcycle sidecar and he hadn't stopped anywhere on the way. 'A serious conundrum', he thought to himself. In fact, he hadn't come across such a conundrum ever since Mrs. B's husband had suddenly gone mysteriously missing over five years ago. It still played on his mind as it was the only conundrum he hadn't solved during his entire tenure as Garda Sergeant in control of Blarnagosha and Poolavogue. A bizarre coincidence then occurred not more than a minute after this thought had entered his head. He answered his doorbell to a woman in her mid-sixties or so who looked a little familiar. She asked if she could come in as she had a private matter to discuss with him. He duly obliged and led her into his small sitting room which was sparsely furnished with just an old but very comfortable armchair. A pungent smell of pipe smoke hung in the air. Gilfuddy invited her to sit in the armchair while he fetched a chair from the kitchen.

'So, what can I do for you, Mrs....?'

'Sorry, I should have introduced myself...Kathleen Higgins.'

Kathleen fetched a piece of paper from her pocket.

'I thought I'd show this to you first as I know you were the Garda Sergeant at the time Tom Brophy disappeared.'

 She handed the letter to him which read....

"Dearest William,

I am telling Mrs B about us tonight and that I am leaving her. I'll see you in Dublin at the arranged placed and time on Wednesday.

Love,
Tom x

The date on the letter was a little over five years old. Kathleen went on to explain that her husband, William, had died three days ago and she had come across this letter when she was looking through some of his private things. She now remembers that he seemed particularly upset for a few months about something around that time but had never discussed it with her.

'I see.... well, sorry for your trouble and I'll certainly look into this...seems a bit suspicious alright.'

After Kathleen Higgins had left, something sprung into his head. It was something that had been playing around the fringes of his brain for five years but had never really settled into a cohesive thought. He had previously dismissed the fact that Mrs B had seemed to recover very quickly from the disappearance of her husband and was able to perform and win the auditions for "Watch the Talent " with apparent ease, putting it down to delayed shock. And was he the only one who'd noticed that she had sung the words, 'blanket underground,' and not, 'blanket on the ground.' and was it even relevant or just his mind playing tricks? Either way, Seamus Gilfuddy had a lot of time on his hands these days and felt he had nothing to lose by looking into the matter again with fresh eyes.

CHAPTER SIXTEEN

Rees Mogg had little difficulty in finding Jockeytown. The directions from the deranged woman with an alter ego of Joanna Lumley were very precise. When you first come across Jockeytown it seems like you are experiencing an optical illusion. It can be likened to entering a film set because there is an air of unreality about it. It is a similar experience to being part of a tour of a faux cowboy town in Hollywood where actors dressed as cowboys are wandering about. You even enter through a small gate to gain access to it. Rees Mogg approached the first jockey he came upon.

'I say, excuse me'

'Jaysus Francie, what do ye think you're doing in Jockeytown, we've no time for you here.'

'No, I can assure you I'm not ...eh...Francie, I'm looking for a chap named Jacko?'

'Well, you need look no further...you're looking straight at him, straight in the face...straight in the face you're looking at him...did anybody ever tell you you're the spittin' image of Francie?'

'Yes, I was told by the lady who runs the B&B'

'Grand, so if you're not Francie Joe, who are you?', he asked in a friendly tone.

For some reason, Rees Mogg hadn't actually thought of an alias. Possibly because he was travelling on his own passport it didn't enter his head. He had to suddenly think on his feet.

'St John Baldwin.' he said very hurriedly.

'That's a very peculiar name…. very peculiar indeed…I would say it's the most peculiar name I've ever heard in the whole entirety of me life.

'Yes, I suppose it's a bit unusual…. anyway, this woman also mentioned that you might have a spare room.'

'That I do but look at the height of you…it used to be my mother's room and she was only 4 feet 7…and she was even small for her size.'

'Small for her size?' Rees Mogg quizzed.

'She certainly was.'

'Well, I'm sure I can manage somehow.'

'Right you be but you'll probably wake up with fierce cramps everywhere on your body…..follow me.'

Rees Mogg followed Jacko down the small street, receiving disapproving stares from a few other jockeys as he went who'd assumed he was Francie Joe. They arrived outside one of the tiny houses. Jacko opened the door and invited him inside. Rees Mogg had to bend his upper body considerably in order to pass through under the door frame.

'Even if you're not Francie Joe, you're still terrible familiar all the same...it'll come to me.....Jaysus, it's come to me.... the old English fella who lives in the last house down the street...you could be his son.'

'Well, definitely not related, I'm afraid...is he a jockey like yourself?'

'Oh God no...came here years and years ago, said he just wanted some peace and quiet.... not short of a few bob either, is he. Had the whole house re-built so he could fit properly into it.'

Rees Mogg noticed what he first thought was a painting hung up on the wall of the sitting room, but it turned out to be a photograph. It was a photograph of a horse racing scene but one of the jockeys had been dislodged from his saddle and was being whisked away into the air by an enormous bird of prey. Rees Mogg studied it closely.
'I thought at first that this was a painting.'

'No painting, I can assure you...that photo was taken at the Curragh racecourse in May 1972. Poor 'ol Scobie, never seen again.'

'Scobie?'

'Scobie Mullen…. the jockey.'

'You mean…he was actually snatched from his horse by a giant eagle and never seen again?'

'I do…the betting industry hushed it up, not the first time it happened either. I could name a list of jockeys who've disappeared over the years.'

'Good Lord…. quite astonishing.'

Rees Mogg went right up to the photograph so that his eyes were less than half an inch away from it. He wanted to see if the photograph could have been tampered with in some way but couldn't see anything in it that would indicate that. Jacko then led him into the miniscule bedroom which used to be his mother's before her death. Rees Mogg saw immediately that only half his body would fit on the bed which was wedged in from wall to wall. He realised that he would need to sleep sideways on
it with most of his legs dangling over the side.

'Well, at least it's only for one night', he thought to himself.

'Right so, I'll let you settle in. I'll tell you what.'

Jacko paused for a few seconds and Rees Mogg felt the need to cover the silence.

'What's that?

'I'll tell you what….'

'Yes?'

'There's a bit of a shindig down in the pub later, Mattie O'Hara's daughter is getting married next week...why don't you come down and join us?'

'Oh, thank you for the kind invitation...not really much of a drinker, to be perfectly honest with you.'

'8 o'clock.... come on down out of that...not often we have a visitor.'

That evening, Vasco sat in his bedroom contemplating his life...going over in his head the sexual shenanigans with Roisin in this very bedroom the night before and whether or not she knew that he was a virgin up to then. His ruminations were interrupted by the sound of his parent's arguing downstairs. This time he could hear them clearly.

'So how long have you been keeping this a secret from me?', he heard his father ask in a booming voice

'Not sure exactly...about six months.'

'Six bloody months......SIX....six months!

'Well, on and off.'

'But...but how did you keep it a secret...why didn't I notice.'

'I was very careful, Gem.'

Vasco heard a thud as his father flung something to the ground and then stormed off up to their bedroom, muttering expletives to himself as he climbed the stairs two steps at a time in rhythm to each new profane utterance. Vasco was devastated...his mother having an affair! and who with?...Jesus!...'

Rees Mogg didn't really know why he'd decided to make his way down to the little pub in Jockeytown later that evening. Maybe it was a combination of curiosity and loneliness. Also, he'd already decided it was probably too late to call on this man named Francie Joe and it would be better to wait till the following morning. Furthermore, he considered that he might garner more information about the pig farmer from people in the pub. "Would he be the only non-jockey in the pub?"

The pub was very small as he'd expected. There were about 20 or so jockeys either standing at the bar or sitting around at tables. The bar counter was set at a height of only three feet, 8 inches. Jacko approached him as soon as he'd entered. Rees Mogg had to stoop demonstrably in order to prevent his head from pressing against the low ceiling in the pub.

'St John, as I live and breathe, come in, come in. People can't believe how much you look like Francie Joe.'

Rees Mogg had never drunk Guinness in his life and would not have expected that he would have a taste for it. However, it would be an understatement just to suggest that he had a taste for it. Two hours later, he had already consumed six pints of Guinness, and in his own words was 'getting stuck in' to his seventh pint. That is not to say that he was not getting a little unsteady on his feet or that his vision was becoming a little blurred. There was animated conversation all around him, but his eyes suddenly settled on an old man sitting on his own in the far corner of the pub. Were his eyes deceiving him and was his normally sharp sense of judgement impaired due to his excessive intake of alcohol.

'By God, it is him...I'm sure of it.' he said to himself almost breathlessly.

He was about to walk over to the old man but then realised that his legs were not obeying the command from his brain.

8th November 1974

(Newhaven, England)

John Bingham parked his car on the coastal road by Newhaven. He didn't bother to clean the few blood stains that remained on the steering wheel and also left the blood-stained oil pipe in the boot of the car once he'd abandoned it. His old Eton school friend, Bunny, had followed him in his own car to Newhaven as instructed by Bingham who stepped into the passenger seat of Bunny's car after he'd locked his own car and thrown the keys over the cliff into the sea.

'Are you going to tell me what this is all about, Johnny, 'ol chap?'

'Not now, Bunny, just trust me, please.'

'Suppose I'll have to.... it's a bloody long drive to Wales from here.'

'I know but it's in the opposite direction to here...it's my best bet.'

'As you wish.... I was there once during the war, Godforsaken place, Holyhead.'

'Yes, so I hear.... I'll put it all in a letter to you in a few weeks once things have died down.'

'Jolly good...Holyhead, here we come.'

They drove through the night and arrived in Holyhead around 6 am. It was good timing as the ferry to Dublin was due to depart at 7.05 am. Bingham kept putting a hand to his expansive, faux red beard to reassure himself that it was still in place. Once or twice during the drive from Newhaven, he'd patted his breast pocket which held his new false passport. It had to be prepared within a few hours and accordingly the faker had charged him more than the standard rate for producing it at such short notice.
He would no longer be John Bingham, or even Lord Lucan, 7th Earl of Lucan, but Alfred Lightfoot.

They said their goodbyes to each other, Bingham thanking Bunny profusely. Bingham walked nervously to the terminal building, carrying just a small suitcase with him. It was cold and bleak inside the terminal building and there were already quite a few people seated inside on the uncomfortable plastic seats, waiting for the ferry to Dublin. Bingham entered the building, his eyes to the floor and picked a seat as far away from any of the others as was possible. However, his chosen spot of isolation from the other passengers was soon to be invaded. A man, sporting a beard similar to Bingham's (although his beard was genuine), strode purposefully across the floor and ensconced himself noisily beside him.

'That's a grand beard you have.' he said to Bingham with a knowing smile on his face, 'take you long to grow it?'

Bingham had never grown a beard before in his life so he had to take a wild guess at how long a beard of his length would take to grow.

'Em.... about three months, give or take',

'Same as meself.... Luke Lannigan, at your service.'

He extended his enormous hand to Bingham, and they shook hands, Lannigan's workman- like hand enclosing Binghams to the extent that you could only see the tips of Bingham's fingers protruding from Lannigan's hand.
'Pleased to meet you...Alfr...Alfie Lightfoot.'

Bingham felt that the abbreviation of Alfred seemed less formal. It felt really strange to him introducing himself with his new name, but he had no doubt that he would get used to it in time. They chatted for a short while, although most of the conversation ebbed from Luke Lannigan who espoused the role of the garrulous Irish man. Bingham occasionally just nodding or injecting a monosyllabic affirmative here and there. Lannigan insisted on accompanying Bingham onto the ship and then invited him into the bar for a drink or two once they'd placed their luggage in the hold. He'd winked playfully when he'd uttered the words...'or two'. A couple of hours into the ferry crossing, Luke Lannigan was in full voice, offering renditions of "The Wild Irish Rover", not just once but over and over again, sometimes forgetting the words halfway through and then starting up again from the start. Throughout, he'd placed an arm around Bingham's shoulder as if they were some kind of a double act, although Bingham didn't attempt to sing but just sat beside him in a state of acute discomfort, faking a smile now and again whenever Luke looked to him for approval of his singing. The ferry crossing took over four hours and Bingham breathed a huge sigh of relief when he saw the buildings of Dun Laoghaire coming into sight from the ship.

He escaped from Lannigan's arm embrace, telling him he needed the toilet and then rushed up to the hold, gathered his suitcase, and placed himself first in line to disembark from the ferry.

Bingham had not had time to work out any kind of plan once he'd arrived in Dun Laoghaire in Ireland. He knew he needed to find somewhere isolated where there was the least danger of his disguise being uncovered. He wandered about Dun Laoghaire while he was contemplating his next move. He was hugely surprised about how British some of the architecture in Dun Laoghaire was, both Georgian and Victorian, and then there was even a 'British' type pier jutting out to sea. He was totally unaware that this is where many British gentry settled when Ireland was still under British rule and many of them had their houses built in the Georgian and Victorian styles. Before Irish Independence, the area had previously been known as Kingstown in deference to the British King at the time. Bingham felt strangely at home in the place and was fleetingly tempted to settle in the area, but he knew such a move would not be wise. It was quite a large port and, in the days, to come, the authorities in England might have cause to snoop around or else ask their Irish counterparts to keep an eye out for him. He didn't think that this was likely, but he had to be careful. He'd been told by a friend that parts of the west of Ireland could be very remote and might suit his purposes, certainly for the time being.

Following some enquiries, he bought a one-way ticket on a train travelling from Dublin to Galway. The man behind the ticket desk was very open and friendly and wondered why he was only buying a one-way ticket. A return ticket was only an extra £2 but a single ticket on the way back would cost him another £8. Bingham told him that he was hoping to settle somewhere in the west of Ireland and spun some story about visiting it on holidays when he was still a child and recalled how beautiful the scenery was and how warm the people were.

'Well now, there's a coincidence. Aren't I originally from

the west of Ireland myself...only left because there was no work there, but it broke my heart. I come from a place called Blarnagosha, a lovely little remote town and some great scenery thereabouts.'

Bingham's mind was made up. He would head straight for this Blarnagoasha place once he arrived in Galway.
The taxi journey from Galway was only about 45 minutes and Bingham was beginning to relax for the first time since 'the incident' at his former home as the lush scenery rolled by. Blarnagosha was indeed quite remote and somewhat isolated from the rest of the world in a way. It was too small to boast of its own tourist office or indeed an estate agent, but he was directed to the local Garda station where he was told the local Sergeant might be able to help him out with his needs. He was slightly reluctant to enter a Police station due to his circumstances but when he saw how small the station was and how isolated the area was in general, he thought it was highly unlikely that he would arouse any suspicion. He entered the small Garda station and was immediately assailed by a pall of pungent pipe smoke.

'Good morning, how can I help you?', a booming voice inquired from somewhere in the room, but the smoke was so thick that Bingham couldn't immediately locate its source.

'Hold on a second, I'll open a window.', the voice continued, and Bingham heard loud footsteps on the concrete floor. As the smoke cleared from the opened window, Bingham saw a man dressed in his Garda Sergeant uniform seated behind a desk, his mouth cosseting a large crude looking pipe from which smoke gushed out in all directions.

'That's a bit better, isn't it.' the Garda Sergeant said jovially.

'Yes, indeed.'

'Do you enjoy a pipe smoke yourself at all.?'

Bingham was about to say that he preferred a cigar but since part of his public persona was associated with cigar smoking, he decided against it.

'No, afraid I don't really smoke.'

'That's a shame…very good for you after a meal, a good long draw on a pipe.'

'Yes, I'm sure. Anyway, I was told you might be able to help me…. hoping to buy a property in this area.'

'Right so, what sort of size would you be thinking of?'

' Oh, just a small holding for myself.'

'I see.'

'My wife died recently.', he lied, 'and I just want somewhere quiet for myself.'

Bunny had advised Bingham that it was always a useful ploy to say that your wife had died recently to avoid any further questioning of your past and present status. People tended to feel slightly awkward and sorry for you once you'd mentioned it and rarely tried to delve any further into your personal life. Bunny had previous experiences of having to remain incognito for long periods in his life.

'Believe it or not, I have the very place for you.'

Garda Sergeant Gilfuddy led Bingham out of the station, turned right and then a further 100 yards down the road he turned left into a narrow laneway. The laneway was bordered on both sides by wasteland, but 300 yards down there was a small cottage, totally isolated and on its own. Gilfuddy showed Bingham around the small cottage. It had a very low ceiling, requiring both men to stoop as they walked around inside it. The cottage housed a small old-fashioned cooking stove inside the sitting room, a bathroom, and a bedroom. All the rooms were very basic but functional although a couple of the windows were shattered and needed repair. There was little furniture in the cottage. A small, tattered sofa in the corner of the sitting room, and a single rickety bed in the bedroom. Bingham noticed a strange sight against the back cushion of the sofa. It looked at first sight like a large ball of fluff but on closer examination, it proved to be a bit more disturbing.

'Is that a dead cat on the sofa?', he asked with some concern.

'Ah, so he came back in the end.'

'What's that?'

'A bit of a story there. The previous owner of the cottage, fella named Christy Delaney, was the owner of the cat. Jasper's the cat's name.... or was by the looks of it. Didn't

Christy up and die about four years ago now and when his body was found by the postman, no sign of Jasper anywhere. Now, Christy had no family apart from a son in Canada. They'd never got on and the son had no interest in taking over the cottage. So, as you can see it fell into a bit of rack and ruin. I can only assume that the cat eventually came back at some point after Christy had been buried, realised his owner wasn't around anymore, fell into a deep depression and just drifted away on the sofa one day.'

Bingham pondered on the matter for a short while. It seemed ideal for all intents and purposes, but would the smell of a dead cat linger forever in the cottage? Surely he could get the place fumigated if necessary. Yes, he would take it and the price was well within his range, althoughhis savings would begin to dwindle quickly. Three weeks later, having stayed in the Mozart Hotel while the cottage was being renovated and fumigated, he moved in. It wasn't until twenty years or so later that Jacko's grand scheme for a self-sufficient new space for jockeys to live in began to take shape. The lane on which Bingham's cottage stood was chosen as the perfect location to build the world's first ever Jockeytown.

CHAPTER SEVENTEEN

(Day 3)

October 21st 2028

Vasco arrived early that morning at Paradise Park. He was still not convinced about the jockey trafficking plot, but he also didn't want to look like a fool if it did become a reality and he was shown not to have acted upon the tip from Jacko. However, as he was arriving at the entrance, he saw the couple under suspicion driving out of the caravan park in their van. Vasco slammed on his brakes, making a loud screeching and made a quick turn in his Ford Escort in order to give chase. The sound of the tyres on Vasco's car screeching on the ground outside his office was sufficiently loud enough for Jerome to temporarily cease polishing one of his shoes and rise from the chair in his office to see what the fuss was about. He opened the door to see Vasco's Ford Escort, fumes steaming from the exhaust pipe, giving chase to the couple in their van.

Vasco didn't have a police siren in the car to warn the couple that he was in hot pursuit of them so he decided to hit the horn in his car, knowing it was faulty and would continue to sound on and off. Not quite a police siren but at least the couple in the van in front of him would know something was amiss and were bound to pullover. He also began to flash his lights at them. However, the sound of the horn blasting intermittently had the opposite effect on the couple. Obviously, they didn't recognise the Ford Escort as being a police car and the sight of its lights flashing and the horn blaring led them to believe that they were being pursued by a local lunatic.

The pursuit lasted over fifteen minutes as the terrified couple tried to shake off the pursuing Ford Escort and the young man behind its wheel.

'What do you think he wants?' Laura, the woman, asked with growing concern as the speeding van struggled to stay on the road while it rounded a bend.

'Fuck knows.', her husband Gerry replied. You can get all sorts in these small towns.

After they'd rounded the bend, they were relieved to see a cattle drover further up the road which was now blocked by a herd of his cattle. They slowed to a halt as they arrived in front of the cattle and the drover acknowledged them with a wave, gesticulating that he would have the road cleared soon. Vasco pulled up behind the van, got out of his car whose horn was still intermittently sounding, and walked up to the van with an air of authority.

Gerry noticed Vasco's uniform as he approached. He was still not re-assured about Vasco as he'd definitely not been driving a police car. He could still be some local madman dressed in a fake uniform. If the drover had not been there, he would definitely have been very worried. Mind you, if the drover had not been there with his cattle, the pursuit would still be in progress.

'Driver's Licence, please.' Vasco requested in a serious tone.

'Before I do that, who the hell are you?'

'Garda Sergeant Vasco Devine of the Blarnagosha and Poolavogue precinct.' Vasco replied, showing him his card.

'Precinct?'

'Precinct.... area...Licence please.'

Gerry fished into his pocket and produced his Driver's Licence. Once Vasco had spent an inordinate amount of time scrutinising it, he handed it back.

'Seems to be in order....thank you...so, rumour has it that you too have an unhealthy interest in jockeys.?'

'Unhealthy.... what.... what do you mean.?'

'I think you might know what I mean.... jockey trafficking is what I mean.'

Vasco didn't say this with a large degree of conviction as he was still doubtful about the whole matter. Gerry looked totally bewildered.

'Jockey trafficking.... are you serious?'

'Deadly.'

A smile then began to appear on Gerry's face as he looked around him.

'This is some kind of prank, isn't it.'

'Nope, I don't have time for pranks.'

'Look…. officer…Garda, I really have no idea what you're on about. We're heading off to the races at Galway and the last thing we intend to do is kidnap some jockeys.'

'So, you won't be heading near Jockeytown in Blarnagosha.'

'Jockeytown….so it does really exist. Heard about it but didn't know if it was true…you hear that, Laura?…that Jockeytown does actually exist.'

'Amazing, we must pay it a visit next time we're round here.'

'You bet.' said Gerry.

Vasco couldn't think of anything further to question them about and let them go on their way. Furthermore, they were heading in the opposite direction to Blarnagosha, so it seemed likely that their story was true. The drover had managed to corral his cattle into the field and the road was now clear. The drover recognised Vasco and came over to talk to him.

'Morning to you, Vasc.... Sergeant.'

'Peadar, how's the world of cattle farming?'

'Oh, can't complain.... can't' complain. What was the story with that couple?'

'Ah, nothing came of it, Jacko tipped me off the other day about a possible jockey trafficking operation in the precinct but probably all in his head.'

'Precinct?'

'Area.'

'Ah, right you be. Mind you I heard tell of two suspicious looking boyos staying over at Mrs B's...Americans apparently but didn't seem like your usual tourists...drivin' a big van as well. Mrs B was saying that one of them doesn't say a word.... the other fella does all the talkin' '

'Interesting.', Vasco said, squinting his eyes as if in deep thought like his hero, Horatio.

'Oh, by the way, Vasco?'

'Sergeant!'

'No, this is not a police matter, just man to man.'

'Okay, shoot.'

'I keep meaning to ask you but then it goes out of my head...

you never refunded me for that ticket I paid for to see Kylie Minogue a few years back.'

'Oh, right...I'll give it to you the next time I see you.'
Vasco replied shiftily and quickly returned to his car to drive back to Blarnagosha.

P J Herlihy and his assistant decided on another tactic immediately following the near disastrous attempt to spear
the "Welcome to Blarnagosha" with the arrow from the crossbow, which could easily have resulted in the death or serious injury to the former Garda Sergeant, Seamus Gilfuddy. They returned to Poolavogue and came back ten minutes later with two shovels. Firstly, they dug up the "Welcome to Blarnagosha" sign and threw it into the nearby field. They then dug up the "Welcome to Poolavogue" sign and moved it 150 yards further forward into Blarnagosha, thus claiming the previously disputed short stretch of land (going back to the time of St. Patrick) for Poolavogue. The land was no use to anyone unless you wanted to grow turnips but it was a statement of intent to Donie Griffin from the townsfolk of Poolavogue.
No one in Jockeytown was suspicious of the two men wandering around the place that morning. Reilly and Jenson planned to carry out 'the operation' later that night and were conducting a serious reconnaissance of the area while pretending to be tourists, taking photos and smiling at the townsfolk.

Jacob Rees Mogg lay sideways in a deep post drunken slumber in Jacko's mother's old bed. He wouldn't remember how he got back to Jacko's house from the pub the night before but would have a vague memory of seeing a man in the corner of the pub on his own whom he thought might well be the infamous Lord Lucan. He'd planned to visit the pig farmer, Francie Joe, early that morning to convince him to make a public statement that it was he in the offensive video and not him. However, he was very unlikely to stir from sleep for some time. A cake of stale Guinness had formed around his mouth while he slept and he was snoring loudly, as he had been throughout most of the night.

Seamus Gilfuddy pulled up on his motorcycle sidecar and parked it on the side of the road just 100 yards or so from Mrs B's B&B. His headless manikin was still sitting upright in the sidecar. He had no particular plan in mind but just felt the need to look around the area. Gilfuddy had already noticed Mrs B earlier standing at the local bus stop awaiting the bus to Galway so he knew that she would not be at home. Mrs B travelled to Galway once a week to visit her hairdresser to have her 'refreshed'. Gilfuddy entered her house by the back door which was usually left unlocked. He felt a bit guilty invading someone's privacy by snooping around their house while they were not there, but he felt it might be justified. He wandered from room to room, opening drawers here and there, looking into cupboards and so on hoping to find something that might give him a clue why Mrs B's husband had vanished for good over five years ago. He found nothing, then left the house and stood outside the door for a while, looking about.

Back at the Garda station, Vasco was feeling a bit restless.

Questioning the couple from the caravan park had led to nothing as he'd suspected it wouldn't. Roisin had taken the day off and he was sitting on his own in the station, twiddling his fingers. He had no idea at this time that this was to be the most frantic day in his short time in the service of the police force. Two hours later, Seamus Gilfuddy arrived at the Garda station. When Vasco saw him walk through the door, he knew something was seriously wrong. The former Sergeant was sweating profusely and parts of his body, including his face and hands, were smeared with soil. He had the look of a man in deep distress.

CHAPTER EIGHTEEN.

When Donie Griffin heard about the "Welcome to Blarnagosha" sign being uprooted and flung unceremoniously into the nearby field, he became apoplectic with rage.

'I'll hang for that bastard, Herlihy, I'm telling ye, I'll bloody hang for him.' he screamed, after the local postman had reported the matter to him.

Ten minutes later he arrived down by the area where the sign had been discarded. Assisted by two other men from the town, he immediately set about uprooting the "Welcome to Poolavogue" sign. However, before he and his helpers had completed the task, P J Herlihy arrived on the scene with his helpers. Herlihy had been training his binoculars on the area from a nearby hillside and had anticipated that Griffin might attempt to remove his sign and return his own one back to where it had been. A standoff between the two councillors ensued. Both in their time had been members of the local Blarnagosha/ Poolavogue Wrestling and Boxing Club and it was agreed that they would engage in a wrestling match with each other to settle the matter. The winner would be allowed to claim the barren 150 yards for his town. It had been raining heavily the night before and the ground on which they commenced battle was wet and soggy. Before long they were both rolling around in the mud, like two Hippopotamuses in Saharan Africa trying to stay cool from the searing sun. It was not clear at what point one of them lost his trousers as they wrestled fiercely with each other. Also, because they were both covered in mud from head to foot, neither was it clear immediately which one of them it was who had been stripped to his underwear. It seemed to be Donie Griffin, but it wasn't clear until he spoke.

'First you ruin my fountain and my flower display and now you're reduced to pulling my trousers off, you dirty no good bowsie.' Donie shouted at Herlihy.

On hearing this Herlihy stood back and seemed a little bewildered. Well, he would have seemed bewildered if you could have seen the expression on his face were it not caked with mud.

'What are you on about?...I didn't go near your fountain or your flowers.'

'You're a bloody liar.'

'I'm not lying to you, ye mad gobshite, I'd never steep that low.'

'If it wasn't you, who the hell was it then?'

'I don't know who the hell it was, but it wasn't me or anyone from Poolavogue.... you have my word on that.'

'Jesus...in that case I'm sorry about the statue. We'll get it fixed and back up in no time.'

'We thought you toppled the statue because you were bitter about Pope Pat 1st visiting Poolavogue and not Blarnagosaha.'

'No, nothing to do with that...did he ever find his hat, did ye hear?

'No, not that I know of.'

With that they both shook hands and agreed to return both the signs to their previous positions and leave the 150 yards of land unallocated to either town.

CHAPTER NINETEEN

Vasco helped the former Sergeant into a seat as he looked like he might be about to faint. Before the Sergeant had a chance to speak, Seamie walked into the station accompanied by his friend, Vinny. He looked very edgy and didn't look either Vasco or Gilfuddy in the eyes when he spoke.

'Eh...listen...it's just.... we have a confession to make.'

'I knew I'd force you into a confession in the end....and you better be able to return every one of those cigarettes today.'

'Cigarettes?'

'Yeah, every one of them or Peadar Scully will skin you alive.'

'It's nothing to do with cigarettes, I didn't steal any cigarettes...it's about the flowers and the fountain, me and some of the lads did it.'

'Is that so?'

'We were just a bit pissed and it got out of hand. Didn't realise it was going to cause a war with Poolavogue.'

'War.... what war?

'Haven't ye heard...Donie Griffin and Herlihy have just beatin' the livin' shite out of each other down by the signs, one of them even lost his trousers during the fight...they shook hands in the end, mind ye.'

'I need to speak to you about something a bit more urgent, Vasco.', Gilfuddy intervened, as he shifted uneasily in his seat.

Seamus Gilfuddy was the only one that Vasco allowed to refer to him by his own name instead of Garda Sergeant in the matter of police business. Vasco dismissed Seamie and his friend, threatening to deal with them later. Gilfuddy told Vasco about the visit he'd had from Kathleen Higgins, about the letter she'd found in her husbands' private papers after his death, and about his discovery of a body.

'You've found a body?', Vasco asked incredulously.

'In her back garden, buried beside the oak tree. It's definitely Tom Brophy, her husband. Remember that hat he always used to wear.?

'Not really.'

'Anyway, the hat was still on his head...never seen a hat on a skeleton's head before...looked very odd.'

'And.... how did you manage to find the body?'

Gilfuddy went on to explain that in the recent rainstorm, some of the roots of the tree had been disturbed and he saw the tip of the hat sticking up out of the ground.

'You mean he was buried standing upright?'

'Looks like it. I think there might have been a well in the same spot there years and years ago and there was a readymade hole for her to slip him into.'

'Mrs B...you think she murdered him?'

'That I do.'

'Hmmm.... murder, Blarnagosha style.' Vasco mused in the manner of Horatio.

'By the way, you haven't seen my mannikin's head anywhere, have you?'

'No, afraid not...is it police business?'

'No, not really.... some bastard ripped her head off.'

Early that evening, Vasco and Seamus Gilfuddy waited at the bus stop for Mrs B to arrive back from Galway. Although

Gilfuddy was no longer there in an official capacity, Vasco had agreed that he could be present when he arrested Mrs B on suspicion of murdering her husband five years earlier and burying his body upright in their garden, since it was he who had found the body. Also, the former Garda Sergeant had agreed that Vasco could take credit for discovering the body as he didn't want to court the publicity. Vasco could feel his heart pumping wildly as the bus from Galway made its approach into Blarnagosha. When Mrs B stepped out of the bus she immediately noticed Vasco and Gilfuddy approaching her. Vasco stood in front of her, his body tensed like a soldier on display.

'Mrs B, I am officially arresting you on suspicion of murdering your husband, Tom Brophy, five years ago and burying him upright in your.....'

Gilfuddy leaned into Vasco and whispered something into his ear. Vasco turned back to Mrs B.

'And burying him in your garden, upright or otherwise... anything you say now will be taken down and used... maybe.... may be used against you in a court of law later, but...not now'

Vasco produced a set of handcuffs.

'Do you have anything to say?'

'Can I just fix my hair before you put the handcuffs on?'

'I can't allow that; you could be concealing a weapon in your hair.'

As Vasco was leading the handcuffed Mrs B into the back of the Ford Escort, Peadar Scully, the pub owner happened to be passing by.

'Jaysus, was it her who stole the cigarettes?', he asked in an astonished voice.

'I'm not allowed to comment on ongoing criminal cases.', Vasco replied with authority.

Mrs B was kept that night in the tiny cell in the Garda station in Blarnagosha, awaiting the arrival of a homicide squad from Galway due in Blarnagosha in the morning. The skeletal body of her long-deceased husband was removed to the nearest morgue, the hat was still in place on his head as it had become wedged to it and the ambulance crew didn't want to force it off in case it might interfere with evidence.

Darkness had descended on Blarnagosha as the two Americans, Reilly and Jenson, drove their van slowly through the main street of the town and turned down the side street leading to Jockeytown. It was after 11pm and there wasn't a sign of anyone out and about. The gate into Jockeytown was never closed and they drove in very slowly, keeping the engine as quiet as possible. They pulled up at the first house, got out of the van and approached the door of the house. From their earlier reconnaissance, they knew which houses were occupied by lone jockeys. They rang the bell. Joey Muldoon opened the door and before he'd had a chance to ask the two men at the door what they wanted, he'd been overpowered, and tape was placed across his mouth to prevent him alerting anyone. He was then manhandled into the back of the van and handcuffed. They repeated this operation three times and there were now four jockeys locked up and handcuffed in the back of the van. They rang the doorbell of the fifth and final house where a lone jockey lived. Jacko answered the door to them. He sensed danger immediately and tried to close the door on them, but they were too quick for him. They followed him into the house, overpowered him like the others and placed tape over his mouth. As they were handcuffing him, another man appeared from a room at the back of the small house. Rees Mogg had suffered such a severe hangover from the night before that he hadn't been able to stir from Jacko's house all day and accordingly had yet to confront the pig farmer, Francie Joe.

'I say, what the…?

However, Rees Mogg didn't have time to complete his shocked query before he too was taped across the mouth and handcuffed. Reilly and Jenson were easily able to wrestle both of them into the back of the van to join the others. They made a quick U-turn and drove out of Jockeytown with five jockeys and Jacob Rees Mogg handcuffed inside the back of the van.

'Who the hell is that other guy…too tall to be a jockey? Jenson posed.

'Damned if I know, buddy. We couldn't leave him to spread the alarm.'

'Maybe he used to be a jockey but never made it to the big time because he was too tall.'

'Huh, maybe. They might buy him along with the others as a kind of 'freak show' jockey.

They both laughed as they sped out of Blarnagosha, heading south.

Seamus Gilfuddy often enjoyed a night ride along the roads of Blarnagosha on his motorcycle sidecar. There was usually no one else about and he would have the freedom of the road to himself, often exceeding the speed limit with his mannikin in the sidecar beside him, her hair flowing and blowing backwards in the wind. This night, however, the mannikin remained headless as Gilfuddy leaned his motorcycle into a bend in the road. Coming out of the bend, he had strayed onto the wrong side of the road and was both surprised and shocked to see the headlights of a vehicle approaching in the other direction.

'What the fuck!' exclaimed Reilly, as he saw the motorcycle sidecar veering straight for them with what appeared to be a headless woman passenger in the sidecar. He immediately swerved to avoid a collision but pulled the steering wheel too heavily and the van hit a small ditch, leaped over it and came to a halt in a rocky field after travelling over the rough surface for twenty yards or so. In the course of colliding heavily with the ditch, the back door of the van had flown open. Once the van came to a halt, the five kidnapped jockeys leaped out of the van, encouraged by Jacko and ran off in the darkness. Reilly and Jenson knew now that their case was hopeless and that the only course of action was to escape in the van without their booty of jockeys before they were arrested. Fortunately for them, the van was still in working order after the accident and Reilly was able to negotiate it back across the small ditch further long and on to the road. They were unaware that Jacob Rees Mogg was still inside the back of the van. He had wanted to escape from the back of the van like his fellow captives, but fear had prevented his legs from moving.

Gilfuddy pulled up on his motorcycle sidecar at the side of the road to allow himself to recover from the shock of his near collision with the van. He'd thought at first that he was imagining the sight of five handcuffed jockeys scampering on foot across the field beside him. He'd then recognised Jacko and called out to him.

Vasco was playing a computer game in his bedroom based on Miami Vice when he received a call on his mobile phone from Seamus Gilfuddy. Gilfuddy told him how he'd come across the five jockeys in a field a couple of miles outside town as they were making their escape from a couple of kidnappers who'd been transporting them to somewhere unknown in the back of their van.

MICHAEL REDMOND

GALWAY COURIER

Monday 22nd February 2024

Garda Sergeant Vasco Devine, of the Blarnagosha and Poolavogue district, has been commended by the authorities for solving one crime and also preventing a major jockey trafficking operation in the area.

Sergeant Devine told the Courier how he'd acted on information received from a reliable source on the disappearance five years ago of local man, Tom Brophy. The body was subsequently found buried near a tree in the garden of the house he shared with his wife known locally as Mrs B. Acting on evidence he discovered at the scene of the five-year-old crime, Sergeant Devine has since charged Mrs B with the murder of her husband. She will be held in custody in Galway until her trial next month.

Sergeant Devine is also credited with foiling a jockey trafficking operation in the area. Two Americans, one known simply as Reilly, and both of whom coincidentally had been staying at the B&B run by the aforementioned Mrs B, had kidnapped five jockeys and another unnamed man who'd been staying in the house of one of the jockeys. Along with former Garda Sergeant of the area, Seamus Gilfuddy, he managed to free the jockeys from the van as it was making its getaway. However, in the confusion that followed, the two Americans managed to escape in the van. The whereabouts of the other unnamed man is still unknown.

The Devine household.

(2 weeks later)

Gem, Bernadette and Vasco, were sitting around the dinner table together.

'We have a bit of news for you, Vasco.', Gem said slightly coyishly.

'I think I already know.', Vasco said, with a tinge of sadness in his voice.

'What...how?'

'You've been having an affair, haven't you, Mum.' Vasco said, turning to look accusingly at his mother.

'An AFFAIR!...me.... what are you on about, Vasco?'

Bernadette looks shocked and deeply offended.

'Have you lost your mind, Vasco.... your mother would never have an affair. What made you think that?

'Well, I heard you both arguing a few days ago and that's what it sounded like.'

'Ah that. I'd just discovered that your mother had secretly been eating vegan food for the past six months.'

'So, is that what you wanted to tell me?'

'Not just that...your dad's agreed to become a vegan as well.'

'Really.... you're actually becoming a vegan.... Gem Devine the vegan.'

Vasco couldn't control the wide grin on his face.

'Not a bloody word to anyone.' Gem threatened.

'Okay', agreed Vasco, 'by the way, I have some news myself.'

'Not another heist, I hope.'

'Roisin is pregnant.'

CHAPTER TWENTY

It was only after they'd arrived at the secluded bay off the coast of Co. Cork that Jenson and Reilly had discovered the overly tall 'jockey' was still in the back of their van. He had immediately begun to protest loudly and demanded to be released immediately. Jenson doused a cloth with some of the chloroform they'd intended to use on the jockeys once they'd hoarded them onto the large rubber dinghy which they'd previously tied up and hid inside a cave off the beach. The dinghy was to transport them all to the ship waiting for them just a short distance offshore.

'Should we do him in and hide the body.' Jenson proposed

'No, killing someone was never part of the plan. We'll bring him with us.... who knows, they might still pay us something for him.'

Three weeks later, Jenson and Reilly learned that the Organisation who had agreed to buy the Irish jockeys off them on delivery to them in Connecticut were not prepared to pay anything for the tall, thin man offered to them by Jenson and Reilly. They abandoned a tired and totally dejected Jacob Rees Mogg on a deserted highway a few miles outside town.

FOOTNOTE:

Jacob Rees Mogg is believed to be presently working as a 'trolley boy' in a Walmart's supermarket in the small city of Providence, near Connecticut.

His doppelganger, Francie Joe, has appeared in another viral video in which he is shown pleasuring himself while sitting naked in a pigsty.

If it hadn't been decided already, the fate of Jacob Rees Mogg is now sealed forever.

Two days after being taken into custody, Mrs B confessed to the murder of her husband five years earlier. He had told her one night that he was in a gay relationship and going to live with his lover in Dublin. She couldn't bear the humiliation of it and as he left the house that night, she'd hit him over the head with an iron bar and then buried him in the garden.

Father Tumelty continues to live in the B&B on his own. Mrs. B had no family so no one took any notice that Father Tumelty was still in residence there. Father Tumelty had had a huge weight lifted from his shoulders following Mrs. B's total disclosure of her part in the murder of her husband to the Police. Following his forced retirement from the role as Parish priest, which he largely blamed on Mrs. B, he had agreed with her that her confession to him about the murder of her husband would remain sacrosanct as long as she offered him free accommodation for life in her B&B.

Vasco and Roisin live with Gem and Bernadette while awaiting the birth of their baby. Vasco still insists on entering the house by the ladder to the bedroom while Roisin uses the front door.

It is not sure if Gem has stuck to a vegan diet. Jacko swears that he spotted Gem one night hiding behind a bush near Peadar Scully's pub, guzzling on a large pork chop.

Lord Lucan has disappeared again.

The Papal MITRE, originally belonging to Pope Pat 1st, sits proudly on the mantelpiece in the sitting room of Seamus Gilfuddys' house. If anyone asks him about it, he claims that it's an imitation....but it isn't.

THE END

.

Printed in Great Britain
by Amazon